BELLA'S BIG
CARIBBEAN ADVENTURE
BOOK TWO

BY ANNE AND ANNABELLE
JOHN-LIGALI

Contents

ABOUT THE BOOK

School is out for the summer and Bella is off to St Vincent and the Grenadines with her mum Isabel, Granny Sylta, Iris, and Tommy. This is not just any holiday, because Bella and Iris are going to be bridesmaids at Clara's wedding, her mum's best friend.

When Bella and the rest of the family arrive at Clara's plush villa in Cane Garden, she and Iris have the opportunity to view their dresses before the big day. The dresses are locked up in a wardrobe that is so old not only does it take ten minutes to open, but you can barely turn the lock.

But after a minor distraction, they miss the chance to view their dresses. Bella and Iris must now wait another week before they can see them. Feeling incredibly impatient, Bella sneaks the wardrobe key to finally have a peek at the dresses. But when a ball sails over the garden wall, the unexpected happens and one silly mistake changes everything and her Big Caribbean Adventure turns into something she could never have imagined.

Bella's Big Caribbean Adventure is a story about the importance of patience, good listening, teamwork, and never giving up.

To the people of St Vincent and the Grenadines

ARTWORK

Cover design and story illustrations: Anne John-Ligali
@anne_johnligali

Cover Illustration: Emily Snape
@emily_snape_illustrator

Formatting: KHFormatting.com

Also By Anne And Annabelle

Book One In The Bella Series
Bella's Christmas Wonderland Adventure

Book Two In The Bella Series
Bella's Big Caribbean Adventure

Bella's Big Caribbean Adventure
Activity And Colouring Book

CHAPTER 1

'It's sunny outside,' Bella called excitedly to her mum, Isabel, while peering out of her bedroom window.

The view looked out onto the street in Notting Hill where they lived. The street was lined with candy-pink blossom trees on both sides of the road.

'The sun makes me feel like I cannot wait for our holiday with you and Granny Sylta,' said Bella, still gazing out the window.

Isabel, who was busy folding a pile of T-shirts smiled. 'You mean your surprise holiday?'

'I wouldn't say surprise exactly.' Bella skipped away from the window and sat on the bed next to her mum. 'I've managed to work out where the holiday destination is. Look, I've got my bucket and spade ready, and

I can't wait to have fish and chips by the sea.' She pointed to the items next to her pink wardrobe.

Isabel laughed, '*Aah*, so you think we're going to the seaside somewhere in England?'

Bella nodded. 'Of course.'

'And what makes you so sure?' Isabel slid Bella's clean clothes into a drawer and closed it.

'Because last week I found the evidence,' she said proudly.

'What evidence?'

'Postcards, fridge magnets, and photographs from our last holiday in Great Yarmouth spread out on your bed.'

Isabel giggled as she left the bedroom with Bella tottering close behind.

'I'm right, aren't I?' asked Bella.

Still not spilling the details about the holiday, they jogged downstairs, heading for the sunny patio where two glasses of cool drinks and a bowl of fruit were set out.

'So, I've got a little detective on my hands have I?' said Isabel, taking a seat.

Bella nodded and folded her arms. 'You sure do.'

'Well, I'm afraid you're wrong. We're going miles away from Great Yarmouth.'

Bella rubbed her eyes. 'Miles? As in hundreds and thousands of miles?'

'Yes.' Isabel poured lemonade into their glasses. 'Why don't you take a guess?'

Bella took a sip of her lemonade and thought hard. She scratched her head. 'So not Southend?'

Isabel shook her head.

'And not Portsmouth?'

Isabel shook her head again. 'A bit further. Guess again.'

'Spain? Turkey? India? Australia?'

Bella's mum laughed and shaded her eyes from the sun.

'Okay, I give up. Where are we going for our summer break?'

Isabel slipped on a large pair of sunshades, and with a smile, she replied, 'St Vincent.'

Bella blinked and paused taking another sip of lemonade. 'St Vincent?'

'Yep.'

Bella squeezed her eyes shut when a fluttery feeling of butterflies settled in her belly. 'Are you alright, Bella?' asked her mum with a curious stare.

Bella broke her silence. 'There's no way I can go, I'm really sorry.'

Her mum placed her drink down on a coaster. 'Why ever not? I thought you would have been excited. This will be your first holiday abroad.'

'I suppose but...' Bella's heart thumped and she gazed up to the sky. Her heart thumped faster when she spotted a plane flying overhead.

'Go on, spit it out,' her mum continued.

Bella took a huge gulp of lemonade. 'I'm worried.'

'For what?'

'The last time I was so high up was when me, Iris, and Tommy got stuck at the top of that humongous ride last December at Christmas. And I promised my-self I would never go up in the air like that again.'

Isabel covered her mouth to stifle her laughter. 'I understand about you being thousands of feet in the air but a plane ride is a far different experience than getting stuck on a fairground ride.'

Bella didn't believe that at all. How could travelling in a plane be so different from being on a fairground ride? Didn't being on a plane meant you'd be even higher and see for miles? Why couldn't mum have chosen somewhere local and easy to get to by train or road? It didn't have to be Great Yarmouth again but Paris or Venice would have been okay.

'There's also a little surprise when we get to the island,' her mum went on.

Bella laughed nervously. 'Which is?'

'Firstly, your friends, Iris and Tommy are coming too.'

Now that certainly was a surprise. 'Are they really?' This piece of news lifted Bella's spirits a little, but not enough to make her forget about being miles above the ground.

'And secondly…' her mum sat up straighter. 'We are going to my best friend's, wedding.'

'You mean Clara?'

'That's right.'

'Oh, I've never been to a wedding or seen a bride in real life before,' said Bella, now feeling a pinch of excitement. 'What a wonderful surprise.' Bella forced a bit of enthusiasm into her voice. She hoped it sounded genuine.

Isabel looked delighted. 'I haven't told you the exciting part yet.'

'Really? There's more?'

'You and Iris are going to be bridesmaids!' Her mum threw both arms in the air.

Bella barely lifted an eyelid. 'Awesome. So not only am I going to a wedding, but I'm going to be a bridesmaid with my best friend at your best friend's wedding?'

Isabel nodded.

Bella sat quietly and looked up at the sky once more.

'Are you not excited? You're going to be bridesmaids.' Isabel waited for a reaction but it never came. 'Most kids your age would be.'

'I know but—'

'Take your mind off that fairground ride. Believe me, when I say, you have nothing to worry about.' Isabel hugged her daughter.

Bella smiled and stood up. 'Okay Mum, I believe you. I need to make a phone call.' She left the patio and raced back upstairs to her bedroom. She couldn't believe Iris and Tommy had never mentioned this trip to her and she wondered why.

Chapter 2

'It was supposed to be a surprise!' laughed Iris, to Bella and Tommy as they did a three-way FaceTime call on their phones moments later.

Bella sat up on her bed and sipped more lemonade through a straw. 'It sure was a surprise guys. What I'd like to know is how come the both of you knew before me?'

Iris grinned from ear to ear, as she skipped towards her bed and sat down. 'Tommy overheard the telephone conversation between his mum and Granny Sylta. Then he called me and told me not to say anything until it was confirmed. So I suppose we're going on holiday then.' Iris rolled onto her side.

'Hmm, I suppose,' Bella said firmly. 'I'll just close my eyes when I'm flying high above the clouds.'

Iris giggled.

'I can't wait,' Tommy joined in as he scooted around the park in Lakersfield. 'This is going to be one huge adventure. Imagine, all those palm trees, blue sea, fresh fish and fruit … it's going to be like starring in the Pirates of the Caribbean.'

Iris nodded. 'Absolutely, but come on Tommy, do you think the grown-ups will let us out of their sight? Let alone have an adventure like that?'

Tommy rubbed his chin. 'I don't see why not; I'm fourteen, and you and Bella are now both eleven. If we stay local of course they'll let us.'

Bella couldn't care less about all that pirate adventure palaver, it was the thought of being so high up, it outweighed everything that made Iris and Tommy excited.

'How cool would it be to take your binoculars, camera, and notebook you got for Christmas,' Iris beamed.

'And me with my inquisitive mind,' added Tommy, and then addressing Iris. 'Hey Iris, I thought you didn't like heights either, how come you're so happy about all this?' he said, grinning at the phone screen.

'Because I have a plan.' Iris nodded with confidence.

'Which is?'

'When we arrive at Heathrow Airport I'm going to ask Isabel to put me as far away as possible from the window seat.'

Bella pursed her lips. 'Seems you've got it all figured out then.'

Iris chuckled. 'It's going to be a wonderful break, and look on the bright side, when we go back to school in September you can show the class all of your holiday treasures like seashells and photos and the beautiful blue sea.' A smile appeared on Bella's lips; she was beginning to warm to the idea, well, just a little.

'And let's not forget.' Iris flicked her fringe out of her eyes, 'It's not like you're going to be the only one on the plane, you'll be up in the sky with hundreds of other passengers.'

Bella placed a finger over her lips and thought about it for a moment. 'You're right, you really are,' she said.

'And lastly,' added Tommy, hopping off his scooter. 'If we are sitting together which I assume we are, you don't need to worry, it's only a seven-hour and forty-five minute flight.'

Bella's nose twitched. 'What did you say?'

Chapter 3

Midway through the flight, Bella covered her entire face with one of her hats to take her mind off the turbulence as they flew high above the clouds. This however made no difference. Even using a blindfold, listening to her favourite band, nothing seemed to work until she decided to research a few facts about St Vincent in a book she ordered online.

She had discovered that La Soufriere volcano had erupted five times; first in 1718, 1812, 1902, 1979, and more recently in 2021. And the most popular place to visit on the island was the Botanic Gardens.

As Bella lapped up the rich history between the pages of her book, she was happy that reading seemed to be the only thing to take her mind off the bumpy ride, and she also knew the Botanic Gardens were a place she just had to go and visit.

***

'Granny Sylta! Look, there it is!' yelled Bella, one hour after their plane had landed and checked out. She pointed to St Vincent's most famous landmark, the La Soufriere as it stood majestically way off into the distance as they left Argyle International Airport in a taxi.

Now with a smile on her face and relieved she had gotten through the worst part of her holiday, she held up her camera and filmed the lush green fields and colourful houses that whizzed past the cab window like a shimmering rainbow.

Granny Sylta tapped Bella on the arm. 'I take it you're happy you came then?'

Bella grinned. 'I sure am,' she said.

Iris and Tommy, who were sitting in the seats opposite beamed.

'I told you you'd be fine, Bella,' assured Iris.

'And I can't wait to explore the island,' chimed in Tommy.

'Me too,' replied Iris.

'And I can't wait to get to Clara's house to finally see our dresses,' said Bella, winding the window down some more to catch the cool breeze. The thought of being a bridesmaid gave her a thrill. 'Oh Granny, this is a dream. Imagine being a bridesmaid on this beautiful island.'

'You wanna bet?' Tommy joked, and everyone laughed.

CHAPTER 4

Clara's house was more than Bella had ever imagined. To say it was just a house was so wrong, it was a villa, a huge one, surrounded by palm trees, colourful birds, and a balcony that ran on for miles.

It had been two hours since they arrived and Clara had shown everyone around and escorted them to their rooms.

Bella was excited after being told she and Iris would be sharing an *en* suite. How organised Bella had thought, not just for arranging the guest rooms so beautifully with tropical bouquets, light calypso music through the entire house and spraying the rooms with fruity air freshener, but for also arranging many of her family and friends to attend a barbecue with music in her huge back garden. And if that wasn't enough, there was a big swimming pool too.

The garden was incredibly busy and with Clara's friends also. They had come over to welcome Bella and her family to St Vincent. Everyone tucked into the self-service buffet of tasty seasoned Caribbean dishes and introduced themselves to each other.

The edge of the pool was lined with pink parasols and sun loungers, and Clara's friends and family who were already there were taking a dip, playing ball games, or relaxing in the shade of the swaying coconut trees.

Like everyone else, Bella and Iris had changed into their swimming costumes and were flapping about in the cool water.

Tommy didn't fancy getting in the pool and instead relaxed on one of the eight sun loungers.

Groups of children played near the pool and ran around on the grass. A few other younger children sat under a tree while a grown-up read them a book, and three girls played racing games with a dog that ran into the garden chasing its tail. The girls and the dog ran back and forth along the length of the pool, while a giggling toddler in a yellow onesie toddled about in a world of its own and chewed on a wooden spoon.

As Bella and Iris swished about in the swimming pool, Bella spotted her mum as she strode out of the house and onto the lawn with a huge smile on her face. Bella noted she had changed into a bright pink kaftan.

'Look, Bella, there's your mum.' Iris pointed.

Isabel headed straight to the poolside and crouched down. 'Girls, I've got something to tell you,' she said.

Bella shaded her eyes from the sun and looked up. 'What's that?'

'Clara's fiancé, Kenneth, has popped out for the rest of the afternoon, so Clara's going to give us a peek of the entire bridal collection, all the jewellery, and your bridesmaid's dresses.'

'Ah!' squealed Bella. 'Can't wait!'

'No way!' yelled Iris and faced Tommy who was now stretched out on the sun lounger face up with his eyes closed. 'Did you hear that Tommy? Wanna come with us?'

Tommy faked a yawn. 'Do I look like a girl?'

Bella laughed. 'Come on, let's go, Iris. I had no idea Clara was going to let us see them.'

'Great,' said Isabel. 'I'll meet you girls inside. I'll be in the room on the ground floor next to the gym.'

Bella and Iris nodded with enthusiasm.

'And don't forget to dry off properly before coming into the house,' Isabel reminded them. 'We don't want anyone to slip on those marble floor tiles,' said Isabel, and sang a happy tune as she strolled back to the house.

The girls swam to the pool steps and climbed out. They grabbed their towels to dry off.

'What colour do you think the dresses will be?' asked Iris, squeezing water from her ponytail.

'Red? Orange? Pink? *Ooh*, I don't care. I'm just happy we're a part of the wedding party.' Bella patted her face with the towel.

Finally dried, they tossed their towels onto one of the sun loungers and skipped across the busy lawn when a bright red football came sailing over the wall and almost landed on Bella's head.

'Hey! Watch it!' complained Bella, frowning.

'I think it came from the neighbour's garden.' Iris pointed.

Bella picked up the ball and threw it back over when a little boy's head appeared over the wall.

He smiled and beckoned Bella and Iris to go over to him by waving his hand.

'What does he want? He's got his ball back,' huffed Iris.

'Have no idea, let's go see quickly, and then we'll leave.'

As the girls neared the wall the boy offered his hand. 'Bonjour, I'm so sorry the ball nearly hit you,' the boy said in French to them, and offered his hand. 'I'm Troy, nice to meet you.'

Bella and Iris looked confusingly at each other then finally accepted his handshake. Bella noticed Troy had a book under his arm and on the spine, it said, *"How to Speak French"*.

'Are you learning French?' asked Bella.

Troy laughed. 'No, it's my hobby. I love to practise with people I don't know.'

The girls nodded and smiled.

'Where are you from? I've never seen you before,' asked Troy.

Iris fixed the strap of her costume. 'We've travelled all the way from London and landed a few hours ago.'

'Yes, we're here for my mum's best friend's wedding, Clara.'

Troy's eyes lit up. 'Cool.' He tossed the ball into the air and caught it. 'I'm going to the wedding too. Clara and Kenneth, right?'

'That's right,' confirmed Bella, shading her eyes from the blazing sun. 'I take it you've known Clara a long time seeing that you're neighbours.'

Troy shook his head. 'Not really, we're new to this area, we used to live in Fancy, close to the Rabacca River, which is the northern part of the island close to La Soufriere. My parents prefer it down here though.'

Bella's eyes sparkled having already read up on the many interesting facts about the volcano.

'So how long are you in St Vincent for?' he asked.

'Ten days,' said Iris.

'That's not long at all, and not long until the wedding.'

Bella grinned. 'Yes, and not long before Iris and I get to be bridesmaids for the first time, and do you know …' Bella paused mid-sentence. A flash of panic across her face. 'Oh no. No-no-no.'

'What's wrong?' Iris asked, worried. 'Are you okay Bella?'

'We forgot about seeing our bridesmaid's dresses, Clara said she was going to show us them and the jew-

19

ellery and shoes and all the pretty accessories.' Bella raised her hands and backed away.

Troy laughed. 'Don't worry, you're going to see them before the big day arrives.'

'I know but I wanted to see them today while Kenneth was out,' explained Bella.

'Aah, I see,' said Troy.

'Quick, we have to go.' Bella galloped across the busy lawn leaving Iris behind.

'Bella! Wait!' said Iris. 'You're so impatient!'

Bella stopped and looked over her shoulder to see Troy laughing and waving goodbye.

'Call me if you need anything! Au revoir!' shouted Troy, as Iris zoomed off trying to catch up with Bella.

Chapter 5

'Where did you both disappear to?' Said Clara, as Bella and Iris dashed into the room where the dresses were kept.

Clara was struggling to twist a key in the lock belonging to a very tall and ancient-looking wardrobe. It was made of thick dark wood and looked exactly like the one in *The Lion, the Witch, and the Wardrobe.*

Bella noticed how the colour of the wardrobe matched Clara's long hair and her almond-shaped eyes.

'You missed everything,' said Bella's mum, eyeing her watch.

'I'm so sorry girls,' Clara popped the key in her pocket. 'But I have to lock it all up now. No one must have access to this wardrobe because not only does it have all the dresses inside, but all the bridal shoes, the

21

shimmering veil, tiaras, silk bouquets, and even the rings.'

Bella wanted to thump herself. How could she be so silly? 'If it weren't for that stupid football flying into the garden I would have seen everything. Now we have to wait until dress rehearsal.'

Clara laughed. 'Speaking of dress rehearsal, there could be one in a few days. So not only will you see your dress, there's a chance you might be able to wear it too.'

Bella pressed her hands together in a steeple. 'Please, pretty please can we have a dress rehearsal?'

Clara laughed again. 'We'll see.'

Iris fanned a mosquito away from her face. 'Can't you open the wardrobe again for us?'

Clara sighed. 'I don't have a problem opening it, the only thing is because no one ever uses this old wardrobe, it took me ten minutes to work the key in the lock and I almost broke a nail.' Clara grimaced at her sore finger. 'So I'd rather not if you don't mind, girls.'

Bella and Iris's shoulders slumped as Isabel guided them out of the room and back into the spacious hallway that smelt of roses.

Clara closed the door and stood on a chair that was next to a shelf with a pink vase. She slipped the key out of her pocket and popped it in the vase. 'There, the key is safe and sound.' She stepped down from the chair and smoothed down her dress. 'I was supposed to have a spare key cut, seeing that is the only one I have. Imagine if it got lost?' she giggled nervously.

'I doubt it,' said Isabel. 'The key is perfectly fine up there on the shelf. No one knows it's there apart from us.' Isabel surveyed the hall in a mock-detective way.

Bella, however, threw Iris a knowing look. Of course, isn't that the point? Thought Bella. No one else knew about the key apart from them. Bella grinned as an idea bubbled in her mind.

As Clara and Isabel made their way back to the garden and continued to chat happily about wedding flowers, the toddler in the yellow onesie waddled past, chewing on a floppy sausage dog toy.

The baby plopped its bum down in a smattering of toys and began to play noisily.

'Never mind,' Iris told Bella. 'There's one thing for sure, you're going to look amazing.'

Bella grinned and rubbed her hands mischievously. 'And there's one thing for sure, we know where the key is which also means…'

Fear crossed Iris's face. 'Don't you dare Bella Matthews. Leave that key where it is up on the shelf.'

Bella tapped her foot impatiently. 'Just having a peek wouldn't hurt. What harm would it do if no one knows? And technically, Clara didn't say we weren't allowed in, she said she did not want to open the wardrobe which means two different things entirely.'

Iris huffed and folded her arms.

'Look, I'll simply unlock the wardrobe, have a quick look, and put the key back. Easy.'

Iris did what she did best and covered her eyes with her hands.

23

To ensure the coast was clear, Bella spied both ways up and down the long hall and edged towards the chair that Clara had just stood on. She climbed the chair, picked up the pink vase, and tipped out the key into the palm of her hand. Bella noticed the detail on the tail of the key. It curled and swirled into a beautiful pattern. She jumped off the chair and down onto the floor, eager to finally see the dresses. 'Got it!' She raised the key in the air with joy.

The toddler stared at them both and burst into a dribbly giggle.

'This is insane,' whispered Iris. 'Why can't you be patient? What if you get caught?'

'I doubt it.' Bella strolled over to the door of the room where the wardrobe was. As she reached for the handle she heard a voice from behind.

'Bella.'

The girls whipped round to see Isabel standing there. Somehow she had walked around a different corner to the one she had left. That was the thing about Clara's house; it had many hidden passageways and fake doors that looked like bookcases and large mirrors, just like houses in the olden days but a modern version.

Quickly, Bella shoved her hand behind her back as her body trembled. She trembled so hard the key slipped out of her hand and landed where the giggling toddler sat, who was now biting the floppy toy dog to pieces. 'Yes Mum, what is it?'

'Clara is cooking corn on the cob and wanted me to find out if you girls preferred it roasted or boiled?'

Bella and Iris released a breath.

'Is that it, Mum?' Bella laughed nervously while Iris remained quiet. 'We'd both love roasted corn, please.'

'Roasted it is.' Isabel smiled and walked back the way she came with the toddler now following close behind.

Yes, it was definitely another secret passage.

Bella and Iris watched with wide eyes after Isabel and the toddler as they left.

'Phew, that was close,' said Bella.

'You're lucky.' Iris batted another mosquito away with the back of her hand.

Bella scanned the entire hall. 'Quickly, let's get the key and put it back into the vase where it belongs.'

Iris raised her hands. 'Hurray, at last.'

Bella crouched on all fours to pick up the key from the smattering of toys but there appeared to be no sign of it. 'Where is it?'

'What?' said Iris, wiping sweat from her face.

'The key.'

'It's on the floor where you dropped it.' Iris dashed over to the toys and rummaged around. 'How strange, it must be here somewhere.'

Bella lifted the toys, one by one, shook them, and moved them around. 'How could it have disappeared? It's supposed to be right here.' She pointed to the exact spot.

Iris rubbed her temples. 'Hang on, the toddler that was sat here not too long ago, what if—'

'The toddler?' Bella laughed. 'Naah way.'

'Yes,' protested Iris. 'She or he, I can't tell, was sat right where the key fell.'

'Are you suggesting the baby took it? Why would a baby take a boring key?' asked Bella.

'Boring to you, but to a baby, it's an interesting shiny shape.'

Bella fell silent for a moment, then in unison, the girls turned and shifted their gazes towards the garden that was still heaving with activity.

They spotted the toddler now sitting next to Tommy, still giggling and surrounded by more toys.

'Come on,' said Bella. 'Let's ask him.'

'A key? With the baby?' asked Tommy, moments later as he played peek-a-boo with the toddler who was now splashing about in a paddling pool wearing only a nappy.

'Yes, Tommy, a key,' said Bella, feeling the pressure of finding it and returning it as soon as possible.

'Sorry, I haven't seen a brightly bunch of coloured plastic baby keys anywhere and—'

'They are not a bunch of coloured plastic any-thing,' butted in Iris. 'It's just one key, a real one. It's silver, very shiny, and has a lovely detail on the tail.'

Tommy bit his bottom lip. 'Does this silver key have a curly tail?'

'Yes.' Bella blinked eagerly.

'You've seen it haven't you?' added Iris, blinking fast.

'Well … yes, I suppose I have based on the de-scription.'

'So where is it?' Bella sat down on the grass with urgency.

Tommy looked at the baby who was now doing snow angel moves on its back and splashing about in the cool water. He said nothing.

'Told you so.' Iris clicked her fingers. 'I told you it was the toddler, who else would the culprit be?'

'But we checked,' said Bella, with a sheen of sweat on her forehead and cheeks. 'It's not here or over by the door where the wardrobe is or where the baby sat even.'

'*Aah,* well…' Tommy stuttered. 'I didn't tell you the other part.'

'What other part?' Bella looked up sharply.

'I had no idea.' He shrugged. 'I thought the key was a toy.'

'What?' Said Iris.

'Get to the point Tommy, my patience is wearing thin.' Bella gritted her teeth.

Tommy sat up and dried his legs with a towel. 'The toddler stuffed the key in the toy sausage dog that he was playing with earlier.'

'You mean that floppy sausage dog the baby was biting to pieces?' asked Bella.

'Yes, I remember seeing him with that toy.' Iris looked around quickly. 'Great! It has to be here then.'

Bella and Iris dropped to their knees and began to rifle through the new pile of toys that surrounded the paddling pool with record speed, but there was still no sign of it.

'It's not here,' cried Bella, breathless.

Tommy grimaced again. 'That's because the sausage dog belongs to one of the local dogs that wandered into the garden when you and Iris were still inside. The dog strolled in, claimed his toy, and left.'

CHAPTER 6

'Mum's going to kill me when she finds out I'm the one responsible for ruining Clara's wedding and for wasting her money on plane tickets,' complained Bella, pacing back and forth the length of the large *en* suite bedroom that she and Iris were sharing at the villa.

The family had just finished having dinner and it was 7pm.

The sound of crickets could be heard from the garden, chirping like millions of tiny alarm clocks going off at once.

Iris folded her arms. 'I'm not going to tell you I told you so, Bella. That'll be rubbing it in.'

Tommy sat up on a chair and arranged one of the pillows behind his back. 'No, go ahead Iris, tell her you told her so, Bella should have never taken that key, now look at the mess she's gotten herself into, and dragged me and you into it.'

Bella flared her nostrils. 'Fine, we can't turn back the clock. No point in dwelling on what's gone wrong, let's see what we can put right?'

Bella was unsure if she closed the window to keep the noise of the crickets out, or because Iris suspected someone listening in to their top-secret conversation.

Iris turned back to her friends. 'So, what's the plan?'

Bella stopped marching mid-pace and sat on the edge of her bed. 'The only plan is to get the key back from that dog thief.'

Tommy laughed. 'Ha! Says one thief to another.'

Iris shook her head at Tommy's insensitive sense of humour.

Bella switched on the air conditioner. 'Tommy, there was something you said earlier that's come to mind. You said the dog was a local dog. Are you for sure and certain? And if so, how do you know?' asked Bella.

'The boy who accidentally kicked his ball over the wall knew the dog's name, which proves it's a local dog,' said Tommy.

'You mean Troy?' asked Iris.

'Is that his name? Well, I suppose so.' He shrugged and became silent when suddenly his eyes lit up. 'Hang on, what if the dog belongs to Troy?'

Iris sat up and blinked. 'Now you talking.'

Bella's eyes flickered, as if something came back to her. 'I think I remember seeing a dog in the garden today.'

Iris took a seat at the edge of Bella's bed. 'Me too, wasn't it the brown dog? The one racing back and forth and playing with those three girls?'

'That's the one.' Tommy stood up sharply.

'It must be Troy's dog then,' said Iris. 'Makes perfect sense seeing that he lives next door.'

Bella pursed her lips in a manner that proved she was not convinced. 'Suppose the dog is Clara's? It was in her garden, right? Suppose the key is in this house?'

'First of all, a dog does not live here,' said Tommy. 'I've seen no sign of it since the family gathering. And earlier, at dinner, I can confirm I overheard Clara telling Granny Sylta she used to have a dog but somebody stole it.'

'Well, that rules that one out then.' Iris shuffled on the bed to make herself more comfortable.

'So back to what I was saying.' Tommy sat down again crossing his legs. 'When you and Bella went into the house to look at the dresses, Troy called the dog. And if the dog does belong to him, the sausage dog toy and key must be with him too.'

'Right next door, right at this moment. Bingo!' yelled Iris, punching the air. 'If he knew the dog's name, of course, it must belong to him. Tommy, you're so great at solving things.'

'Indeed,' chimed in Bella. 'And informing us the dog is a local dog is a great tip-off and moves our investigation in the right direction and one step closer to finding the key.'

Iris tilted her blonde head, confused. 'Investigation?'

'Yes. Our big Caribbean adventure has now turned into a sausage dog investigation.'

'But there's nothing more to investigate. Based upon what Tommy said the dog and key are next door.' Iris sprung to her feet. 'We can go there right now.' Iris made off for the bedroom door and reached out and twisted the door handle.

'Wait!' Bella looked at her watch. 'Let's call on Troy first thing tomorrow morning. He's probably getting ready for bed.'

Iris released the door handle and skipped back over the bed..

'And once we get the key,' Tommy sat up with a satisfied smile. 'You can put it back in the vase like nothing ever happened.'

'Well, let's hope so,' said Bella. 'because no key means no dresses, no dresses means no wedding, no wedding means Mum will kill me, and then I'll be grounded; she'll confiscate my phone, she may even sell our West End tickets for a show I've been dying to see since I was five, and for the next six months I'll be burdened with litter picking duties in our garden, and my neighbours garden.'

Tommy pulled a face and shook his head. 'Jeez, your mum's savage.'

Iris flicked her blonde fringe out of her eyes and blinked at Bella with curiosity. 'But if your mum kills you, wouldn't it be impossible to do litter picking duties?'

Tommy belly laughed and threw his pillow at Iris.

CHAPTER 7

The next morning, after breakfast Bella told her mum she, Iris, and Tommy had made friends with Troy, the boy next door, and wanted to visit.

'Troy?' asked Bella's mum as she helped Clara and Granny Sylta clear the breakfast things off the table. 'Oh, how lovely you've made a new friend already. Are you planning to do anything nice?' her voice was light and bubbly.

'Sightseeing.' Bella knew there was a slither of truth in that. Visiting the sights in the hope they spotted the dog. 'Yes. The island is so beautiful I thought I'd take the opportunity to take pictures, use my binoculars and reporter's notebook I got for Christmas to soak up some local culture.'

Isabel grinned so widely Bella thought her mum's face was going to split. 'Well, well, to say I'm impressed is an understatement.'

Bella laughed but her heart sank at the thought of all those beautiful wedding clothes and shoes locked up in the wardrobe.

'What time will you and your friends be back home?' asked Isabel, now washing up the dishes.

'Oh, hopefully, we won't be too long, say around 3 pm?'

'Okay. Have fun with Troy and be careful,' her mum said.

Chapter 8

Troy's yard was rich in vegetation of all kinds and colours. Abandoned toys lay across the path and an old picnic table with a few used paper plates and cups sat in a shady corner of the garden.

As Bella and her friends shuffled their way through the yard, they heard a voice call out from somewhere in the large tree canopy above.

They looked up and spotted a red T-shirt and a wide smile. It was Troy.

With the expertise of an Olympian, Troy climbed through the branches, down the trunk, and jumped to his feet. He dashed over to the three friends with a smile. 'Bella and Iris, nice to see you so soon,' Troy greeted, then acknowledged Tommy with a nod.

'Oh, this here is our friend, Tommy, who also travelled with us from England,' Bella introduced. 'He was in the garden too that day.'

'Aah, I see.' Troy and Tommy shook hands. 'So what brings you to my door? Not that I'm complaining,' he chuckled.

Bella adjusted the sun hat on her head. 'Your dog. That's what's brought us here.'

Troy looked puzzled. 'My dog?'

'Yes.' Iris stepped forward. 'The dog you called over to your side of the wall when your ball landed in Clara's garden yesterday.'

Troy's eyes shone with recognition. '*Aah*, that dog,' he laughed again.

Bella's face lit up. 'Yes, can we see him? Does he still have his toy sausage dog? Is he around?' She tilted her body sideward to look past Troy. Her eyes scanned the narrow hallway in case the dog walked by.

Troy shook his head. 'That's not my dog.'

'What?' Bella's heart quickened.

'But yesterday you called the dog over,' said Tommy. 'What name did you call him then?'

'I called him dog,' said Troy.

Iris's shoulders flopped. 'Dog?'

'Uh-huh,' he grinned, folding his arms.

'So if you don't know the dog, why did you call it over?' asked Bella.

'Lunchtime leftovers. These St Vincent dogs have supernatural appetites. They can eat a whole village if you let them.' Troy giggled, but stopped when the others didn't laugh back. 'Am I right in suspecting something's wrong? What's so important about the dog, may I ask?'

As fast as she could, Bella updated Troy on the key and wardrobe situation, and how the toddler slipped the key inside the toy that belonged to the dog who had walked off with it, and now Clara's wedding and Bella's freedom was at stake.

Troy's eyes widened to the size of two large coconuts. 'You seem to be in some hot Caribbean pepper sauce. Rather you than me my friend.'

Bella huffed at his comment. If one more person reminded her of her silly mistake, she'd scream. 'Great, so now we're trying to find a dog with no name. So if we spot the dog, we can't even call him.'

'Him?' asked Iris. 'It could be a she though.'

Tommy covered his mouth to stop himself from laughing.

'We could try whistling to get the dog's attention if we see it,' suggested Iris.

Bella plopped her sunshades on the top of her head. 'So this means the case has run cold already. Great. My life. Is over.'

Everyone was silent as Bella's words hung in the air.

Bella gazed up towards the sunny sky. 'How could this be happening?' she asked herself. 'We had better be going home then. No point in hanging around.' She gave Troy a weak smile. 'Thanks for everything.'

'Pleasure.' Troy nodded with sadness.

The three friends turned and left the yard when Troy called out to them.

'Stop!' He ran over. 'Actually, there is one thing I remember about the dog.'

Bella's eyes ignited and so did her friends.

'The dog had a tag around its neck and I remember seeing a name on it. It begins with a G. What was it again?' Troy clicked his fingers as Bella and her friends waited patiently, then suddenly his eyes lit up. 'It said Greiggs. That's it.'

'Great.' Smiled Iris. 'Now we know the name of the dog. He's called Greg.'

'No, that's not his name and it's pronounced as Gregg, but spelled with an 'I', so Greiggs,' explained Troy. 'That's the name of a village out in the country-side. I strongly believe that's where the dog is from. It's common for some Vincentians to tag their dogs with the name of the village where they live.'

'Was there a phone number on this tag?' asked Iris.

'Even if there was, would he remember?' said Tommy.

'Actually, there was a phone number,' added Troy. 'But no, I didn't take notice of that. But as Tommy said, I would have never remembered it.'

Tommy shifted aside to stand more in the shade under a mango tree as sweat ran down the side of his head. 'So where is Greiggs in relation to where we are now? In fact, where on the island is this place we're staying in relation to anything?'

Bella shrugged off her rucksack, unzipped it, and pulled out a large tourist map of St Vincent and a red pen. She headed over to the abandoned picnic table and the others followed. She spread out the map as everyone gathered around her. 'Right Troy, where are we on this map?'

Troy took the pen and pointed to mark the spot. 'We're in the area of Cane Garden, the southern part of the island. Greiggs is not all that far. It's going up north and slightly east from here. So you're lucky.'

'Can you show us where Greiggs is on the map?' asked Tommy.

Troy slid his finger across to the spot.

Iris fixed her cap on her head to block out the blazing sun. 'How long do you think it will take for us to get there?' asked Iris.

Troy bit the inside of his mouth. 'With all the stops in between, by bus, it should take about forty minutes.'

'And by cab?' asked Bella.

Troy released a breath. 'By cab, maybe twenty-five.'

Bella closed the map into a neat rectangle and gave a satisfying smile. 'Well, by cab it is.'

CHAPTER 9

'Camera and binoculars.'

'Check.'

'Packed lunch and cool water.'

'Check.'

'Umbrella and raincoats.'

'Check.'

'Mobile phones and chargers.'

'Check.'

Bella, Tommy, and Iris ticked off their list of the things they needed before setting off to Greiggs and were thankful to Troy for his tip-off into the sausage dog investigation.

'Are you sure that's everything?' asked Iris, as they headed towards the local taxi rank just five minutes from Clara's house.

Bella quickly scanned the list again when something tingled her attention. 'Ah-ha! Money. We have no money.'

Tommy smiled smugly and pulled out a wallet from the back pocket of his shorts. He flipped it open to reveal a thick wad of Eastern Caribbean Dollars.

'Where on earth did you get all that money?' laughed Bella, as they slid into the smooth cool seats of the first vacant cab.

'Remember those prizes I won in the Puzzle Room at Christmas Wonderland last year?' grinned Tommy. 'Well, let's just say I made a killing on eBay.'

Iris chuckled. 'Tommy Smith, I'm so proud to be your best friend.' She hugged him, but Tommy playfully brushed her off.

'Right,' said Bella, tucking the list away into her rucksack. 'That's everything covered then.'

'Looks like it to me,' said Tommy, shoving his wallet back into his pocket as the cab drove away from Cane Garden.

CHAPTER 10

The drive to Greiggs was not as long as Troy's estimate. Instead of twenty-five minutes, Bella had timed it to take just fifteen minutes.

The closeness of the destination put Bella at ease as they were, after all, in a foreign country they'd never visited before. And although Tommy had his 12th birthday a couple of months ago, and Bella and Iris were now eleven, they were still young, but not too young to have a bit of freedom.

The cab took them to the heart of Greiggs and, like a gentleman, Tommy paid.

As they stepped out of the cab, Bella felt overwhelmed at the sight. She wasn't sure if her friends felt the same too.

'Any ideas of where to start?' asked Iris, taking in the bustle of the colourful market and shouts from traders.

'Not sure,' replied Bella, gazing around.

Tommy rubbed sunblock on his arms and face. 'I'm trying to fight the feeling that this might have been a bad idea coming all this way expecting to find a dog with no name.'

'Please don't say that, you're worrying me,' panicked Iris.

There was one thing Greiggs was not short of, and that was dogs. There were dogs everywhere of every kind, colour, and size.

'St Vincent people really love their dogs, that's for sure,' observed Bella, and smiled at one that jogged past with its floppy tongue hanging out of its tiny mouth.

'Agreed,' joined in Iris. 'Out of all the dogs hovering about, neither of them look like the one we're after. We don't even know the breed.'

'I'm sure Troy will know, we can ask him later. Come on, let's wander around and see where that takes us,' suggested Bella.

They wandered through the market, passed a flurry of fish stalls, danced along to Soca music blaring out from buses with passengers inside until they reached a busy street that was lined with brightly coloured houses. The houses were not as big as Clara's, they were bungalows.

It was a pretty sight of colours and an interesting chorus of sounds from people selling all sorts. The fruity smells of mango drifted from bowls spread out onto tables, shady palm trees above swayed like huge umbrellas, and the fresh cool sea breeze offered relief from the blazing sun.

Steelpan music blared from a local shop selling handmade Caribbean wooden sculptures and post-cards, and a plump woman who wore a pink head wrap sold Caribbean patties, chicken, and bread from a huge bucket.

Tommy sniffed the air. 'I know breakfast was a few hours ago,' he glanced at his watch. 'But does any-one fancy brunch?'

Iris laughed. 'How can you think about food at a time like this?'

Bella rolled her eyes. 'He's a boy, what do you ex-pect?'

The three kids headed over to the lady and bought enough food and drink to keep them full until dinner time.

Tommy paid the smiling lady. 'This is a lot of food. We ought to find a park where we can sit down and eat it. There's no way we can walk and talk with all this food in our hands.'

'Good idea,' said Iris.

They spent the next ten minutes trying to find a park and finally spotted one filled with people sitting with friends while others played music.

'Perfect, let's sit over here,' suggested Iris, pointing to a shady spot under a palm tree.

The friends followed her lead, sat down, and be-gan to eat.

Chapter 11

Twenty minutes later, all three friends had eaten and were glugging back their drinks.

It was clear to Bella that Iris had ordered too much as she laid lazily on her back with her eyes closed hardly able to budge an inch.

'That was almost as nice as Granny Sylta's patties and coconut dumplings,' Iris admitted.

'You bet,' said Tommy, draining his can of Vitamalt and sneakily reaching for another.

'I regret not buying more,' said Bella, 'but we can't all be little piggies now, can we?' she giggled when her phone buzzed on the grass. 'Oh God, it's a video call from Mum. Do you think she'll be able to tell we're not in the area?'

'Of course not,' Tommy huffed. 'One palm tree looks pretty much like another. Why are you panicking anyway? She knows we're out and about. Just answer the phone.' He shook his head with slight annoyance.

Bella took the call and her mum's smiley face appeared on the screen.

'Ah, Bella, how's everything?' smiled Isabel. 'Just checking you three are okay. How's the sightseeing going? Good?'

Bella glanced wide-eyed at her friends when Tommy silently mouthed, "Just say the truth that it's going well."

'It's going well,' Bella laughed nervously. 'We're chilling in this beautiful park and had a bite to eat.'

'A park?' asked Isabel. 'How wonderful. I may come and join you seeing that you're local. How far away from the house are you?'

Far away? What? Bella wanted to pass out. Local? No-no-no. She couldn't let her mum know she was miles away in Greiggs. She'd freak out. 'Mum, I have no idea which park we're in.'

'Not to worry, Clara will know the names of the parks in the area. We can come and join you with some food and drinks. How about that?' smiled Isabel.

Bella looked at Tommy again, who was no longer telling her to "tell the truth."

'Thanks, Mum, but that won't be necessary. We're leaving to come home now so we'll be home in five minutes,' Bella said quickly. She felt awful, adding another lie to the biggest lie of all. And it was all her fault.

'That's perfect because I spoke to Clara and she said she doesn't mind opening the wardrobe again to show you and Iris the wedding clothes.'

Bella froze, and Iris sat bolt upright from lying on the grass after hearing what Isabel had said.

'Hello? Bella? Are you there?' said her mum.

Bella gathered herself. This was too much. First, the park and now worst of all, to open the wardrobe that had no key! Bella's heart raced as the obvious consequences and chaos pushed her into a corner. 'Mum please, tell Clara not to bother opening the wardrobe. It doesn't mean as much as it did before. I promise.' Bella stared at Iris. 'Isn't that right Iris?'

With wide eyes, all Iris could do was nod while Tommy shook his head.

'Are you sure sweetie? Because Clara doesn't mind at all, she said it will only take ten minutes to open the lock.'

Bella patted her chest. 'No, please. I don't want to be a bother, really.'

Isabel displayed a mock sad face. 'Okay then sweetie, if you say so. When you get home you can fill me in on how your day went, yes?'

'Uh-huh,' said Bella and hung up quickly. She stared into the sky willing for this horrible situation to disappear.

Iris threw an arm around her friend for comfort. 'Don't worry Belles, we'll solve this mystery, no one will know the key is missing, Clara will have the wedding of her dreams and… and…oh … my God….' Iris's voice faded.

Bella looked at Iris to find her friend's eyes had magnified as Iris stared straight ahead.

Tommy also studied Iris and gazed in the same direction to find out what had caught her attention.

'Oh my God,' said Bella, standing up.

'Am I seeing things?' said Tommy.

'No, that's him alright,' added Iris.

The three friends couldn't believe what they saw. The dog with no name was sitting beside a woman who wore a broad-brimmed hat.

The dog rolled around in a bed of flowers without a care in the world, and in its mouth was the toy sausage dog.

Chapter 12

The kids couldn't pack the leftover food packets and cans of drink into their bags fast enough.

'Quick! They're leaving,' yelled Tommy, gearing up to run.

The dog and the lady were headed towards the park exit.

Bella swiped her camera from her bag and quickly took a few snaps of the dog to forward to Troy so he could confirm the breed.

The dog skipped out of the park gates and trotted down the busy main street with its owner.

This was a challenge for Bella and her friends who had to dodge a flurry of people, food carts, traders, and more dogs.

'Troy was right,' Bella said to her friends. 'It's a Greiggs' dog alright.'

Iris swiped a baseball cap from her bag, popped it on her head, and wiped her face with a damp flannel. 'I hope I don't pass out in this heat.'

'Keep an eye on him, we can't lose him now,' said Tommy, dodging three women carrying large bowls of coconuts and fresh lemons on their heads.

The dog continued to hobble down the road and took a few corners here and there, passing more dogs of the same kind and smaller dogs until suddenly the dog and the woman stopped by a stall.

'They're buying ice cream,' said Iris.

Tommy squinted in the blazing sunlight. 'That's not ice cream, that's snow cones. And now's our chance to approach them and retrieve the toy.'

The woman stood second in line as she watched the snow cone vendor pour lashings of tinned milk over the fruity ice.

Tommy licked his lips. 'I could do with one.'

They waited for the woman to pay before making their move.

Bella studied her for a moment, taking in her huge St Lucian T-shirt. She leaned in close to her friends and lowered her voice. 'She must be a tourist like us.'

Tommy nodded. 'I was thinking the same thing, because of her T-shirt,' he said.

She bought two snow cones and gave the dog one while she ate the other.

The dog took a seat next to the woman's feet and dropped the toy sausage dog on the ground so he could eat the tasty dessert.

'Oh!' Bella shrieked. 'Let's get it now.'

Tommy reached out and grabbed Bella's arm. 'Wait, we can't just rush in, we must have a conversation.'

They watched as the dog's owner slurped through a straw and the dog lapped his up greedily on the ground.

Tommy gave the nod. 'Let's go for it.'

They shuffled forward and Bella made the first move. 'Erm, hello,' she said, in a small voice.

The woman turned and caught Bella's eye. She said nothing.

Bella pointed to the dog. 'Sorry to bother you but may I take a look at your dog's toy? We have a dog just like yours and we're thinking of buying him a toy dog too.' Bella's eyes were fixed on the toy lying on the ground and lowered herself to pick it up. 'He's such a lovely dog, isn't he?' she smiled.

The woman stared at Bella suspiciously.

Tommy and Iris tensed as they held their breaths.

Bella was now inches from the toy. 'You're a good boy, and so lovely and—'

'Excuse moi!' the woman said, astonished.

Bella jumped back and gasped. 'I'm so sorry.'

The woman carried on. 'Que fais-tu? Lache-moi, chien voleur! Va-t'en!' she ranted.

Iris gazed alarmingly at the woman.

Tommy rolled his eyes up to the sky. 'Great, she speaks French. That's all we need.'

'Which explains the St Lucian T-shirt,' said Iris in a shaky voice.

Bella tried all she could to calm the lady by raising her hands, however, this did nothing, she still ranted in French.

'I'm so sorry,' Bella pleaded. 'I didn't mean to startle you, I was only asking to look at the toy. I don't want to steal it,' she begged, close to tears.

Tommy stepped forward with his hands on his hips. 'Madam-mooze-zell,' he said, in an awful French accent.

The woman ignored him.

The dog had finished its snow cone and they both decided to move on at a much faster pace down the busy road.

Iris tried to keep up with her friends. 'Does anyone know how to say "key" in French?' she asked.

Tommy shook his head "no" then suddenly skidded to a stop. 'Iris, well done.' He patted her on the back so hard she misbalanced.

'Well done for what?' she asked, rubbing her back.

Tommy whipped out his phone and typed into the English to French Google translator.

He typed: *"We don't want your dog, we only want to see inside his toy, there is a key inside and we desperately need it. Please. Trust us."*

'That ought to do it,' said Tommy, trying to catch up with the woman and dog again.

'Quick! They're slipping away,' cried Bella as the woman and dog sailed past a stall selling green bananas and disappeared around a corner. 'She has to read it.'

The kids raced around the corner too and spotted the woman and dog crossing a busy road.

'There they are!' Tommy yelled as they zipped to the other side of the road only to meet a herd of cows that blocked their path.

'Oh, look at these cows,' complained Tommy. 'Get out the way.'

'There's millions of them,' said Iris, pushing her way through.

'Come on, let's try to weave in and out. We can't lose them.' Bella led the way and maneuvered around them. It was a lot trickier of a task than saying it, as the cows bumped and brushed their warm smooth skins together.

A cow jerked Bella to the side with its bum, another licked Iris's cheek, while Tommy got sniffed by another.

'Poo! Those cows.' He fanned his face. 'What a pong.'

Finally, they made it to the other side and realised the dog and the woman had vanished.

'Where are they?' cried Bella.

Iris swiped Bella's binoculars from her bag and lifted them to her eyes. She looked left then right and choked, 'I've spotted them. There, in the bus station boarding a bus.'

The kids flew across the road, dodging scooters, bikes, and pedestrians. Many horns honked all at once as the busy traffic whizzed all around them.

The bus boarded by the woman and dog began to pull out, but luckily the doors were still open.

'Please don't leave now, we've almost made it,' Bella pleaded to herself.

Tommy sprinted past Iris and ran up to the bus when the automatic doors closed in his face. 'No! Wait! Open!' he cried.

Tommy peered inside and spotted the lady and the dog sitting next to a window. He positioned himself so he was level with the window. 'Read this!' he yelled and lifted his phone high enough for her to read the Google translation. "We're not dog thieves!"

On seeing the message the woman narrowed her eyes as she read it, then laughed.

And just like that, the bus drove off at a speed that was impossible to keep up, even when running.

'What now?' asked Iris, out of breath.

'We jump in a cab.' Tommy pointed to a short queue where three taxis were lined up. He scurried across the road heading for the taxis leaving Bella and Iris behind.

'But we don't know where the bus is going,' Iris looked on with worry. 'What do we tell the cab driver?'

'Who cares?' said Bella, dragging Iris by the arm and in the direction of the taxis,

All three jumped into a cab and Tommy sat in the front. 'Okay driver,' he said. 'Follow that bus!'

CHAPTER 13

Bella and her friends kept a watchful eye on who entered and left the bus at each stop, and at no time did the dog and the woman get off.

'So where did they vanish too?' asked Iris annoyingly, as the cab pulled up behind the bus at the final stop. She folded her arms. 'I'm disappointed. We should have gotten them.'

'It's not our fault none of us can speak French,' Tommy scoffed.

They got out of the cab and scanned the entire street. This end of town was much quieter compared to where they had come from.

Bella stomped over to a lone bench and sat down. 'I can't believe how close we were.'

Tommy's mood softened and he took a seat next to Bella. 'Look on the bright side, we may not know his or her name yet, but for certain it's a Greiggs dog,' he said, offering some hope to the hopeless situation.

Bella smiled a little. 'You have a point and I'm grateful for Troy providing a lead. We'll have to come back tomorrow.'

Iris said nothing and looked at Tommy nervously.

Bella noted the sudden shift in mood. 'Guys!' Bella stood up quickly. 'Are you thinking of giving up now? How about the wedding? The clothes? And everything else?' Bella's voice wobbled.

Iris moved to Bella's side. 'We're not giving up. I just thought you might wanna take a break tomorrow. That's all.'

'A break?' Bella looked horrified. 'The wedding is days away, Mum and Clara still have no idea the key is missing; how can I take a break?' Bella sobbed into her hands.

'Oh Bella, I didn't mean to make you cry.' Iris threw her arms around her friend as Bella trembled against her.

Tommy patted Bella's head as his way of comforting her. 'We had better take a cab home, it will soon be dark.'

Chapter 14

'Masie is delighted to be a bridesmaid,' laughed Clara as they sat around a large dining table in a humongous dining room later that evening.

On the walls were pictures of Caribbean beaches, a huge portrait of someone called Chief Joseph Chatoyer, and in the centre of the room hung a sparkling chandelier that twinkled in the soft evening breeze.

Bella and her friends believed they were in trouble after they noticed several missed calls from Bella's mum.

Isabel asked Bella why it had taken her so long to return since she FaceTimed her in the park.

Stumped for words, Bella didn't have a clue what to say until Troy strolled into the kitchen and saved the day. In his hand was the red pen she had left behind on his picnic table and wanted to return it. Troy's unassuming alibi was perfect timing.

There were lots of chatter and laughter around the dinner table as everyone tucked into their plates of curried mutton and rice.

Kenneth had a warm smile, a button nose, a head of rich dark hair, and he knew how to dress.

Bella thought he was cool and admired his Nike T-shirt, and trainers.

Kenneth passed a large plate of stewed goat meat around while Isabel poured lashings of homemade creamy mango juice into everyone's glasses.

Tommy helped himself to more ice cream while Iris took a second serving of rice.

The baby in the onesie, Clara's baby, who wore an orange onesie, sat in a highchair kicking its chubby legs and biting into a carrot stick.

Granny Sylta shuffled into the room wearing a huge Caribbean shirt dress, paired with pink flip flops. She carried a tray of golden crispy coconut bakes with swirls of steam rising out of them.

Mmm. This made Bella's belly grumble. She couldn't even begin to imagine how awesome those coconut bakes would taste, especially being made with real fresh Caribbean coconuts from the trees in Clara's back garden.

Granny placed the tray of bakes next to Bella and smiled. 'Go on Bella, tuck in,' she encouraged.

Bella pinched four and plopped them on her plate.

'I can see Masie now,' Kenneth joined in Clara's conversation moments later. 'She'll be skipping down the aisle and doing her usual little dance.' He laughed, and so did the grown-ups.

Bella raised her eyebrows at the mention of the word Masie again. Just who was this Masie? And if she was supposed to be one of the bridesmaids, why had she or Iris not met her yet? Perhaps she ought to ask. 'Clara? Who is Masie and where is she?'

Clara put her drink down and smiled. 'Masie is a little darling and I couldn't imagine the wedding going ahead without her.' Clara broke off a piece of cassava bread and ate it. 'Mind you it's been a while since I've seen her.' Clara looked at Kenneth. 'When was the last time you saw Masie?'

Kenneth sat up. 'This morning actually. She was booked in to have another fitting to make sure her dress is perfect for our big day.'

'Aww, darling,' said Clara.

Bella was still keen. 'Why don't you phone her?'

Clara laughed. 'That would be impossible be-cause—'

'Waaaah!' the baby in the highchair dropped the carrot stick and began to cry.

Clara pushed her chair back quickly. 'Oh, there my baby, come to mummy, don't cry.' Clara picked up the carrot stick and tossed it in the bin. She replaced it with another and the toddler giggled.

Tommy scooped up the last spoonful of ice cream and gave his belly a satisfying pat.

'Everyone I forgot to mention.' Clara took her seat again. 'Tomorrow they'll be a wedding rehearsal at the church.'

Iris's eyes lit up with excitement. 'Wonderful, will we see our dresses?'

Bella dropped her fork and kicked Iris under the table.

'Ouch!' yelled Iris, then quickly covered her mouth after realising what she had said. She rubbed her leg.

'Dressing up would be a great idea, Iris,' said Clara.

Tommy looked up nervously and tightened his lips.

'I'm not sure that's a great idea,' Kenneth joined in, spooning hot pepper sauce onto his huge Jackfish. 'Who does a wedding rehearsal in full dress in this hot weather? And besides, we only have five days to go, let's just wait for the big day to get all dressed up.'

Bella perked up on hearing that. 'I agree with Kenneth,' she said quickly and quite loudly.

'Bella, I'm so proud of you,' her mum said. 'And how you've suddenly and miraculously become so patient about wearing the dresses compared to when we first arrived.' She grinned. 'What is it that's changed your mind?'

Bella stared at Tommy and Iris, who was not making any attempt to say a word. If only mum knew, Bella thought sadly.

'And also,' Kenneth went on, 'Isn't it bad luck for the groom to see the dress before the wedding?'

Clara rolled her eyes playfully. 'I was only planning to wear the veil, but okay, you win.' She kissed him.

Clara, Kenneth, Isabel, and Granny Sylta discussed the wedding in more detail as Bella toyed with her food. She pushed a piece of plantain around on her plate with her fork and was desperate for someone to change the subject. She couldn't take anymore.

'Please, no more wedding talk,' said Clara among the joyful chatter.

'Yes, let's talk about how our day went,' suggested Iris, clapping her hands.

'Good idea.' Bella's mum wiped her mouth with a napkin. 'Tell me, kids, how did your sightseeing go? And what park were you in when I video called earlier?'

Bella closed her eyes. She wanted to scream. If only she had left the key alone. If only she had listened to Iris who begged her not to take a peek at the wedding clothes, then the feeling of complete dread would not be taking over her life. Instead, she would have been enjoying her stay in St Vincent, quality family time with no feelings of anxiety or whether she would see that dog again. Oh…that dog. How could she do this to Clara? And all because of her impatience and poor listening.

Bella's eyes filled with tears but she wiped them away quickly before anyone noticed.

She pushed her chair back and stood up. 'May I be excused? There's something I must do.'

The grown-ups stopped talking sharply.

'Oh Bella,' said Clara. 'Are you alright?'

Bella nodded sadly.

'You're tired.' Isabel smiled. 'I can tell from your eyes.'

Tommy and Iris stood up also and asked to be excused.

Quietly, Bella left the dining room with Tommy and Iris following close behind.

Chapter 15

'Are you sure this is going to work?' Iris asked, as Bella pulled out a wad of cream paper from a box in Clara's plush home office.

Bella fanned out the paper like she had seen her mum do many times just before printing. She slotted the paper into a fancy laser printer. 'How will we know if we don't try?' replied Bella.

'Well, I have high hopes it will work,' said Tommy. 'Hope is all we have right now. Thank God you took a photo of the dog. Who knew your photo would have been so useful.' Tommy rested his feet on Clara's office desk as he finished playing a game on his phone.

After returning to the villa, the three friends marched into Troy's yard to update him on their investigation and showed him the picture of the dog.

Troy confirmed it was the same dog that came into the garden, and he was for certain it was a pot cake dog which was a common breed on most Caribbean islands.

It had been an hour since they left the grown-ups at the dinner table and had been working hard to come up with the perfect flyer.

The three friends had brainstormed on how to pin down their "wanted dog" and what important information to include.

As the humongous printer rumbled into life, Bella pressed the send button and printed one copy to check for any changes or mistakes.

The printer lit up, made a flurry of interesting noises and a single sheet of paper swished out and landed on the printer tray.

Bella grabbed it and all three friends read it.

HAVE YOU SEEN THIS POT CAKE DOG?

WE BELIEVE THIS DOG IS A GREIGGS DOG DUE TO ITS COLLAR TAG, BUT WAS ALSO SEEN IN THE AREA OF CANE GARDEN. ALSO, THIS DOG USUALLY CARRIES A TOY SAUSAGE DOG IN ITS MOUTH. IF YOU SEE A DOG THAT FITS THIS DESCRIPTION, PLEASE CALL US, BELLA, TOMMY OR IRIS, AS SOON AS POSSIBLE ON OUR NUMBERS BELOW AT ANY TIME OF THE DAY. THANK YOU.

'Brilliant!' said Tommy, as he high-fived Bella.

'Good job,' complimented Iris. 'However, there is one thing you can add that would make it better.'

'Which is?' asked Bella, admiring the flyer.

'I think you should add a reward, you know, for a bit of motivation?' Iris suggested.

Tommy slapped his forehead. 'Why didn't I think of that?'

Iris rolled her eyes. 'Because you can't think of everything, Tommy.'

'Well, I love that idea,' said Bella. 'Only thing is, what would we offer up for a reward? We have nothing.'

Tommy racked his brains; his eyebrows wriggling again, which proved his level of focus. 'I know!' He clicked his fingers. 'Troy!'

'Troy?' asked Bella.

'How can Troy be offered up as a reward?' Iris shook her head. 'Wouldn't that be illegal?'

'Don't be silly,' laughed Tommy. 'He said we ought to give him a call if we need help, right?'

'But we've just asked him to confirm the breed of the dog, and now you want to bother him again?' said Bella.

Tommy swung his legs off the desk and sat forward on his chair. 'Bella, we're not bothering him, he's trying to help, and it's free help, so take it. Besides, it's your freedom at stake, remember? Not mine and Iris's.'

Bella rubbed her temples. She didn't need to be reminded. 'So how exactly can Troy help with a reward?' she asked him.

'Look at that massive breadfruit and mango tree in his front yard? What if he helps us by offering the person who finds the dog six months' supply of mangoes and breadfruit?' Tommy pushed his chest out with pride.

'Brilliant!' Iris clapped and hopped on the spot.

Bella, however, frowned. 'That's not a good reward at all.'

Tommy released an exaggerated breath.

'And why ever not?' Iris waved the flyer in the air.

'Let me show you something.' Bella ran over to the office window and pulled back the blinds. 'Look around you, there's breadfruit trees everywhere and in nearly everyone's garden. That would be like gifting an Eskimo a year's worth of ice.'

Iris gave that some thought. 'Or, offering a barrel of honey to a beekeeper?'

'Precisely!' Bella thrust her hands behind her back and marched to and fro across the office like a Detective Chief Inspector.

Tommy's cheeks flushed with a tinge of pink. 'Okay, I see how silly that idea is now. So what do you suggest?'

Iris drummed her fingers on the desk as Bella continued to pace the length of the room when suddenly she stopped. 'I've got it!' said Bella.

'What, what, what?' said Iris excitedly.

'Money,' said Bella. 'People love to be rewarded with money.'

Iris's excitement dipped. 'Where do you expect us to find money?'

Bella nodded in Tommy's direction, remembering his wallet stuffed with notes.

Tommy noticed how both girls stared at him with wide grins. He lifted his hands in surrender. 'Okay, okay, I'll offer a cash reward of three hundred British pounds. Happy now?'

Bella grinned. 'You bet I am.'

Chapter 16

It was another cloudless sunny day and, as promised, everyone, including the Reverend Peters gathered at the church for wedding rehearsals. There was certainly a buzz of joy in the air.

Bella wouldn't exactly call it a church, it was a cathedral, St George's Kingstown Cathedral on Grenville Street. Bella would say it was a medium-sized building, not as big as St Paul's back home in London, but it was big enough. Clara must know a lot of people if she were to fill a church this big.

Inside the building felt like an oven. Bella scanned the area desperate to switch on an air conditioner, but she couldn't see one.

'Bella, look,' said Iris. 'They must be the other bridesmaids.' Iris pointed to five smiley girls who carried plastic bouquets in their hands. One of them looked like she could be the matron of honour as she had the biggest bouquet and seemed slightly older than the rest.

Bella tapped Iris on the shoulder. 'We have no practise bouquets like those other girls over there.'

Iris studied the girls. 'One of them must be Masie.'

Bella nodded. 'You're right.'

'Let's go over and introduce ourselves to them.'

As the girls headed straight to the giggling group of bridesmaids, someone called out to Bella from the back of the church.

'Bella! Over here!'

Bella and Iris turned to see Troy with a huge smile on his face.

He was dressed in another red T-shirt but not the one he had worn the other day, this one had a different design. He must like red.

Troy ran over to the girls with a sparkle in his eyes and in his hand was the French book he was studying from. 'Hello girls, have you seen Tommy?' he asked, looking around.

Iris spotted him strolling through the main doors and into the church. She called him over. 'Tommy! Over here!'

Tommy walked over casually with his hands in the pockets of his denim shorts.

'Hi Troy, hi girls,' Tommy said, smiling at everyone. 'I was outside admiring the architecture.'

Everyone laughed and Iris shook her head.

Troy raised his hands like he had something important to say and lowered his voice. 'Any update with the sausage dog investigation?'

Bella and Iris shook their heads.

Tommy shrugged. 'Nope, not a sausage.'

'It's nice to see you. Troy, we weren't expecting to see you here today,' Iris told him.

'And I wasn't planning on coming, but I thought I'd share some important information I discovered about the dog.'

'The dog?' Bella widened her eyes and so did Tommy and Iris.

'I came here to tell you I'm one hundred percent sure I spotted our furry friend.'

'You did?' said Bella.

'When?' asked Iris.

Troy looked around to check no one was within earshot. 'Yesterday, down by the local beach, at Villa, during lunchtime.'

Tommy ruffled his hair in thought. 'Did you follow it?'

'I did, the dog was with a lady wearing a St Lucian kaftan,' said Troy.

'That was her alright.' Tommy sniffed.

'So where did they end up?' asked Bella.

'I'm not sure because they boarded a minibus and drove out of town.'

'Drat!' exclaimed Bella.

'As for the dog,' said Iris. 'Are you sure it was the same one? Wasn't it only the other day in Greiggs? And now by magic, he's showed up here?' Iris was not won over.

'Well, that's what I thought.' Troy sat down on one of the pews.

Tommy's eyebrows began to wriggle again. 'Did the dog have the toy sausage dog in its mouth?'

'Yes, it did.'

Bella gasped. 'No way.'

'Yes, way.' Troy nodded.

'I suppose that confirms it was the dog you saw,' said Iris, fanning her face with her hand and taking a seat. 'This is certainly a game-changer.'

Bella took a seat next to Troy too. 'Okay guys, to-morrow, here's what we do. As early as possible, from eight o'clock, we'll get up and head down to Villa beach where Troy saw the dog and hand out the flyers we made last night.'

Tommy and Iris will stand at either end of the beach, and I'll stand in the centre, just so we don't miss anyone. Deal?'

'Perfect,' said Iris, standing up.

Tommy nodded his approval.

'Will you help us, Troy?' Iris asked him.

Troy looked uncertain. 'I would but I promised my dad I'd help him paint the side of our house tomorrow. But any day after that, and I'm all yours.' He grinned.

CHAPTER 17

'Have you seen this dog?' asked Bella, as she handed out flyers to the locals who bustled to and fro along the sandy path at Villa beach early the next morning.

Numerous strangers swiped the flyers out of her hand while others ignored her and went on their merry way.

The lush green hills, flowers, and a huge pirate ship had just pulled into the bay, and the distant hills of Bequia rose out of the sea which added to the beauty.

'Please, if you can help, it's very important we find this dog and he was last seen on this beach yesterday.' Although it was early, sweat ran down the sides of Bella's head as the Caribbean sun sparkled in the cloudless sky and the sea breeze offered her a little comfort from the heat.

Lifting her hands to shade her eyes, Bella peered across the beach in both directions to check on her friends.

Tommy had stopped a group of fishermen and was eagerly explaining the details on the flyer, while in the other direction, Iris continued to pass them out and was sticking one of the flyers on a shop window.

An hour into handing out the flyers, neither of the friends had spotted the dog, or received any hopeful leads, despite the large number of dogs wandering around on the sand, catching shade under palm trees or lounging under abandoned parasols.

Despite the situation, Bella was in awe and almost believed she was on the movie set for Pirates of the Caribbean.

Bella had never been to a place so beautiful, well, apart from the Christmas Wonderland Theme park last December, but this was on a different level, it was a dream oozing with culture, smells from Caribbean food, a flurry of interesting accents, and she marvelled at how the sun took no time to set, unlike England where the sun would linger and play with the sky until ten o'clock at night, and this made Bella's heart lift. However, when her thoughts drifted to the lost key, the dream fizzled and popped into a nightmare.

Tommy and Iris had just finished handing out the last of the flyers and jogged back towards Bella.

'How hard can it be to spot a dog with a toy in its mouth?' said Tommy, swiping three hydro flasks that contained cool coconut water from his backpack and passing one each to Iris and Bella.

'Hopefully, that should do it. We should get some phone calls anytime from now.' Bella glanced at her watch and clipped her old school mobile phone, the one her cousin Rita gave her last year, to the waistband of her shorts and gave it a tap. 'Great.'

'And let's hope the cash reward of three hundred British pounds will prompt the locals to search for our furry friend,' said Iris, wiping sweat from her face as the Caribbean sun thumped like a hot pulse on her head.

Tommy reached for Bella's binoculars and lifted them to meet his eyes. He swivelled from left to right, scanning the busy area. 'Have you noticed the dogs that live here are different to the ones back home?'

Iris shrugged. 'How do you mean? They all look the same to me.'

Tommy made an inquisitive noise. 'I don't mean that I mean how they take themselves for walks, wander the streets alone and you never see anyone walking them on a lead.'

'And let's not forget the doggie outfits that people like to dress dogs up in back in the UK.' Iris giggled. 'They're all quite independent here, aren't they?'

Bella gazed around at all the dogs too. 'Yes, I agree.'

'Which explains why our little furry friend wandered into Clara's garden and no one questioned whom he belonged to,' concluded Iris.

'Furry friend?' Bella frowned. Some friend she thought.

Bella studied the dogs too as they strolled in and out of beach huts, sat with other dogs, and walked together in groups like they were all a part of a little dog community; meeting up with their friends for a sunny morning stroll. Bella laughed to herself. She couldn't believe it. It was the first thing she had laughed at since the key got lost. She never thought she could laugh again at anything.

The entire morning had passed and now it was almost lunchtime.

They all decided to return to the house with no luck.

As they walked into Clara's sun-baked yard, they spotted Troy next door helping his dad paint the house just like he promised.

Troy was covered in paint and waved a paint-splattered hand at them as they strolled past.

As they entered the house, through the lobby area, the smell of Granny Sylta's fresh-baked bread drifted down the hall.

Iris inhaled the scent. 'I'm really hungry now.' She patted her tummy.

Surprisingly the entire house was quiet, compared to when they first arrived and had been full to the brim with family members and friends.

Bella heard voices coming from somewhere when Isabel, Clara, and another woman she had never seen before walked around the corner.

'Hello kids,' smiled Isabel. 'You guys back so soon? I thought you were going to be out all day?'

Bella blew a raspberry. 'So did we, but we decided to come back early. It's so hot.'

'Yes, we did,' chimed in Tommy.

'For lunch,' added Iris, who licked her lips.

Bella smiled up at the woman she'd never seen before and wondered if she was Masie. 'Are you Masie? One of the bridesmaids?' Bella asked.

Clara laughed. 'No, this is Lucy, my wedding planner.'

Bella, Tommy, and Iris's eyes ballooned out of their sockets.

'Wedding planner?' Bella stammered.

'Yes, she popped in to discuss a few last-minute details before the big day.' She laughed again but louder.

Bella heard herself gulp. 'Last minute details? As in the dresses in the wardrobe?'

Clara shook her head. 'No, not the clothes. The clothes are fine and locked away safely.'

Tommy and Iris exchanged relieved looks.

'Lucy wanted to discuss the music band we're going to hire and the reception details,' said Clara.

Isabel turned to Clara and Lucy and joyfully said. 'How about a Soca band?'

'Or how about a steel pan band?' suggested Clara, wiggling her hips.

All three women chuckled loudly.

Bella and her friends failed to see the funny side, fearful of what likely loomed ahead; a wedding with no clothes.

A surge of fear filled Bella's gut and imagined her friends felt the same.

Isabel stopped laughing and gave Bella a curious stare.

CHAPTER 18

Thirty minutes later Bella and everyone sat in the back garden having lunch underneath a large pink parasol.

Kenneth was not there this time as he had to go for a last-minute suit fitting which gave Clara the chance to talk about wedding stuff to Lucy, in more detail.

Although Iris was going in on her homemade mango veggie wrap, and Tommy helped himself to countless glasses of freshly squeezed passion fruit juice, Bella noticed they focused on their phones and kept glancing at them in case anyone called about the dog.

Bella too couldn't keep her eyes off her phone, itching for someone to call.

'So, tell me, Clara,' said Lucy, placing her napkin on the table. 'Are you sure Masie knows what to do on the big day?' she laughed.

Bella's ears pricked up again.

'Oh, she certainly does,' replied Clara. 'As soon as Kenneth proposed, we began practising with her immediately.

Bella stared at them as she spooned strawberries and mango cubes in a bowl. How come whenever they spoke about this Masie girl they always laughed, or no one would ever give a straight answer when they were questioned about her. Bella still wanted to know who she was, but couldn't be bothered to ask again. After all, she would find out soon enough when the wedding day arrived and would have to apologise to everyone for not having any clothes. Bella cringed inside.

'You're so organised,' complimented Lucy. 'Masie so deserves to be a part of your wedding.'

A fly zipped past Bella's ear and she batted it away when her phone buzzed on the tabletop. It was a message from an unknown number.

HELLO BELLA, MY NAME IS FREDRICK. I'M RESPONDING TO YOUR FLYER ABOUT A MISSING DOG? WELL, I HAVE A POT CAKE DOG IN MY AREA THAT FITS THE DESCRIPTION OF THE DOG YOU ARE LOOKING FOR, AND HE HAS A TOY. AT THE MOMENT I AM ON YOUNG ISLAND AND WON'T BE HOME UNTIL TOMORROW, SO YOU CAN POP ROUND ANYTIME AND GET HIM. I LIVE IN MESOPOTAMIA, SEE MY ADDRESS BELOW.

P.S. MY HOUSE IS GREEN WITH A PINK PORCH AND IS OPPOSITE A YELLOW STANDPIPE.

Bella shook with excitement and dropped her fork with a clatter onto her plate. She picked up the phone and in silence showed the text to Iris and Tommy.

Iris and Tommy's eyes lit up and they punched the air with joy.

CHAPTER 19

HELLO FREDRICK, THANK YOU SO MUCH
FOR GETTING IN TOUCH. MY FRIENDS AND
I WILL BE AROUND FIRST THING
TOMORROW MORNING. YOU HAVE NO IDEA
WHAT THIS MEANS. THANKS AGAIN!!!

Bella screamed into a pillow as the three friends gathered in Tommy's bedroom half an hour later.

The whoosh of the water sprinklers on the huge lawn outside filled the air, and again, Iris closed the bedroom window.

Bella wasn't sure if she closed the window because of the noise, or, in case anyone overheard their conversation while strolling by.

'You were right Bella, I'm sorry I doubted whether your flyers would work.' Iris sat on her bed.

Bella smiled. 'That's fine. The most important thing is we've had a response and tomorrow the missing key will be missing no more.'

Tommy rolled onto his front and stretched out on his bed. 'I always believed in the idea of having a flyer,' he said smugly to Iris, who stuck her tongue out in return. 'However, I was not expecting such a quick response and especially not from someone so far away from here.' He sat up with the map in his hand. 'It's not local at all, which means another cab ride.'

Bella jigged with excitement. 'Oh Tommy, I don't care. We're going to get the key.'

Tommy smiled. 'Yes, we are, finally. Maybe I'm just overthinking. Don't mind me,' he said and sat up on the bed, studying the map once more.

***

'Congratulations!' bellowed Troy, as Bella and her friends filled him in with good news about the dog an hour later.

As soon as lunch was over, they had rushed over to Troy's house.

Troy was finishing his lunch too and slurped heartily on a big bowl of callaloo soup and flour dumplings. 'And look here.' Troy pointed to Fredrick's address. 'You're in luck, he lives in Mesopotamia, which is closer than where Greiggs is from here.'

'Great!' yelled Iris.

'I can't believe it,' said Tommy. 'What are the chances, hey?'

'Tell me about it,' replied Bella, full of smiles.

Troy lifted his big bowl of soup to his lips and drank the rest until the bowl was dry. 'Do you need me to come with you guys?'

Bella shook her head. 'There's absolutely no need now, the case has been solved.'

'How I wish we could go now,' said Iris. 'If *only* Fredrick was available today.'

Tommy sat on another chair too. 'Never mind that, we should be celebrating with cups of coconut juice.' He paused to take a happy deep breath. 'Main thing is … we've got our dog. Bella's freedom is no longer at stake, and the wedding has been saved.'

CHAPTER 20

'Are you sure Bella?' complained Mum, as she made a large batch of avocado and cucumber sandwiches in the kitchen.

She wrapped them in a sheet of cling film and added them to a pile of sandwiches she made earlier. 'I know I didn't ask if you wanted to go to the beach to-day, didn't think I had to,' said Isabel. 'I thought we'd all have a picnic.'

Bella sensed her mum's mood and this made her heart sink a little. She shifted uncomfortably on the high stool next to the breakfast bar in the spacious and spotless kitchen. She felt awful. Her poor mum's high hopes were quashed, but how could Bella explain that today was the day to catch Fredrick at home. Bella could not think of any excuse other than what she had told her moments ago.

'Mum, I'm really sorry, but my friends and I have to be somewhere this morning. It's so important.'

Isabel tore off a piece of cling film and wrapped a large slice of banana pudding she had baked last night. She had also prepared slices of roasted and boiled breadfruit, bags of colourful popsicles that her mum froze overnight. Bags of tambran, seasoned barbecued corn on the cob, barbecue chicken, and a large pot of ox-tail soup.

Oh, God. Why had mum gone through all this trouble? Bella looked at all the food spread out on the tabletop like it was a stall at a food festival. Why did the timing have to be so wrong?

Iris and Tommy were still upstairs getting ready and had yet to have breakfast.

Isabel sat next to Bella on another breakfast stool. The kitchen was quiet with only the two of them.

Bella sensed her mum wanted to say something.

'Bella, is something wrong? You would come and tell me if you had any problems, yes?'

Bella blinked. 'Mum, I'm fine.'

'I hope so because I've been studying you a lot. You've been acting strange ever since we arrived on the island.' Isabel watched her daughter intensely.

Bella scratched her ear lobe. What could she possibly say now? How she wished Tommy and Iris would burst into the kitchen.

Isabel sat quietly and waited for a reply.

'Don't worry Mum, we're here for a wedding.' Bella forced a smile, but Isabel continued to stare.

'Okay,' said Isabel, standing up. She placed both hands on her hips and looked at the food with pity. 'All this food. What a shame.'

Bella wanted to cry and wished she could go back to the day she slipped the key in her hand and had listened when Iris begged her not to, then none of this would have happened. She would have been doing normal things with her family.

'Mum,' said Bella softly, feeling heartbroken. 'I promise, I'll make it up to you. All the days we're not spending together, I'll make sure I do something special with you soon. I'm so sorry.'

Isabel strained a smile and ruffled Bella's pigtails. 'It's okay. You go off and do what you have to do. The island seems to have brought out your adventurous side. And I'm happy for that.' Isabel gazed at the view of the huge garden outside the window. 'At least being here makes up for not having a huge garden to play in compared to the one back in London. So, you go and make the most of it, at least you're enjoying yourself and staying safe.' Isabel smiled.

Bella nodded and slipped off the breakfast stool when they heard footsteps racing down the stairs and along the hall.

Tommy burst into the kitchen followed by Iris, the pair grinning like Cheshire cats.

Isabel laughed. 'My my, you all seem to be full of energy this morning.' Isabel turned to Bella. 'I see that whatever it is you have to do must be really important.'

Bella nodded and grinned cheekily.

CHAPTER 21

This time Bella and her friends travelled by bus. The entire journey to Mesopotamia took just twenty minutes despite the morning traffic and people going to and from work.

After leaving the bus they realised, according to the directions Fredrick had given, they were half a mile away from the street he lived on and this encouraged Bella to walk with a spring in her step.

Tommy walked a few paces behind her and seemed fascinated with this part of the island, peering at everything including the architecture through Bella's binoculars.

Iris, who was almost level with Tommy continuously wiped her sweaty face with a wet flannel.

Ten minutes later Bella stopped when she saw the yellow standpipe Fredrick had mentioned in his message. 'We should be here now.'

They looked around and the neighbourhood buzzed with life.

'How do you know which house is his?' asked Iris.

'He said his house is green with a pink porch and directly opposite a yellow standpipe,' replied Bella.

'Well there's the yellow standpipe,' said Iris, pointing.

'And over there is the house.' Tommy nodded his head towards a house of the same description. 'It must be that.'

Bella's breath quickened with excitement as she and her friends power-walked up to the house and skipped gleefully down the garden path.

Tommy sniffed the air greedily. 'Mmm, is that spicy chicken?'

Iris nudged Tommy in his side.

They reached the door that was left wide open, which was a common thing people did on the island during the day.

Bella called out. 'Hello? Does a Fredrick live here?'

Immediately, a skinny boy around eighteen years old wearing a Spiderman T-shirt and ripped jeans appeared with a huge smile on his face. 'Aah, don't tell me, are you Bella?'

Relieved, Bella smiled brightly, and so did her friends. 'That's right,' she said. 'I can't thank you enough, you have no idea what you've done to my life.'

Fredrick laughed loudly. 'No problem. That is perfectly okay.'

Tommy stepped forward. 'And what a miracle.'

'A miracle?' said Fredrick, looking slightly confused.

'Well, yes. Considering the dog has been spotted in different parts of the island,' explained Tommy.

'Like where?' Fredrick asked.

'Cane Garden, then locally at Villa beach, Greiggs, and now here in Mesopotamia. What a miracle!' Tommy rejoiced.

Fredrick furrowed his brow and rubbed his chin.

'So, in your message, you said you have a pot cake dog in your area, where is he then? asked Bella. 'All we need is his toy as there's something important inside.'

Fredrick rubbed his chin. 'Aah, well he lives here.'

'With you?' asked Iris.

'Yup.' Fredrick nodded. 'Let me call him.'

Feeling excited, Iris leaned in close to her friends and whispered. 'I knew the dog was a boy.' She grinned, and Tommy rolled his eyes.

Fredrick motioned for Bella and her friends to follow him round to the back of the house that gave way to a bushy garden with grass so tall it was almost Tommy's height.

Fredrick called out to the dog. 'Casper! Oh, Casper!'

Iris laughed. 'What do you know? His name is Casper. Such a lovely name.'

'Casper! Come here, boy!' Fredrick continued when suddenly the tall grasses at the bottom of the garden began to move. Fredrick turned to face Bella and the others. 'He's a bit shy, loves playing hide and seek in the grass which is why my dad left it so tall for him to play in.'

The tall grasses began to swish wildly as the dog no doubt sensed their presence and a new smell.

'How exciting,' boomed Iris. 'We'll soon have the key and Clara's wedding will be saved.'

Tommy gave Iris a side glance but said nothing and focused his eyes back on the swishing grass.

Fredrick whistled. 'Come on boy, come on here, come on.'

The tall grass stopped moving, then suddenly the dog moved slowly then rushed forward and leaped out of the grass to reveal itself.

Fredrick grinned. 'Here he is, your missing pot cake dog.'

Bella, Tommy, and Iris stared at the dog in silence. Bella looked Fredrick in the eye. 'This is not the dog we're looking for at all.'

Iris blinked uncontrollably. 'Oh God,' was all she could say.

Tommy sighed and folded his arms. 'I knew it. I knew something was off from the moment I saw the location of this place on the map.' Tommy shook his head.

The dog, a mini greyhound, jumped on its hind legs like it wanted to dance. However, it did have a toy alright, a stuffed octopus that looked like it had gone to war and back.

Bella fought to keep her cool and addressed Fredrick again. 'This is clearly not a pot cake dog, it looks nothing like the dog on our flyer, and that toy he's playing with is an octopus.'

A look of shame flickered on Fredrick's youthful face. 'I'm sorry guys, I assumed you'd want any dog and I was willing to give him away.'

Iris opened her mouth in shock. 'You don't want your dog? Why?'

Fredrick shrugged. 'My dad is too sick to look after him and I'll be going off to university soon.' He patted Casper's skinny head. 'I just didn't want Casper to end up being a street dog. There's so many of those here already.'

Bella nodded. 'That's the only true thing you've said since we arrived.'

'And,' Fredrick continued. 'The reward money seemed very attractive indeed. Three hundred British pounds? Are you kidding me? That's exactly one thousand, one hundred and ten Eastern Caribbean dollars and seventeen cents.' He grinned up to the sky as if to thank God.

Bella, Tommy, and Iris all exchanged the widest of wide-eyed glances.

'That money would cover at least four months' rent for my room at university,' Fredrick continued. 'With a little left over for groceries, perhaps one trip to the cinema and a new shirt.' He grinned.

Iris stared at him. 'I see you did the maths, as they say.'

'Look, Bella, guys, I'm so sorry.' Fredrick stroked Casper on his back. 'I thought you wouldn't have minded at all because—'

'Because what?' Bella interrupted. 'I could have spent the morning or the day with my mum. My poor mum made such a huge fuss and made so much food.' Bella shook with anger as it rose within her. 'I let her down because of your stupid text message, and your lies,' her voice trembled uncontrollably.

Tommy and Iris looked on concerned and edged closer as if they sensed Bella may kick-off.

'How dare you lie to me and let us come all this way to Mesopo-whats-its-face?'

Iris leaned in and whispered. 'It's Mesopotamia.'

'My freedom is at stake, a wedding may get cancelled, there's no clothes, no key, and Clara's happiness will go down the drain.'

Fredrick tilted his head. 'Clara who?'

'And you present us with a dog called Casper? A Greyhound?' she said sharply.

Tommy stepped in front of Bella in a protective manner. 'We need to go. I think we've wasted enough time.' Tommy put a supportive arm around Bella, and Iris did the same. 'I understand you need money for your studies and you don't want Casper to be neglected, but there are better ways to go about solving your life problems.' Tommy looked at Bella, who had now burst into floods of tears.

Fredrick looked as though he may cry too. 'I'm so, so, sorry,' he stuttered, but it was too late. Bella sobbed uncontrollably in Tommy's arms and Iris rubbed her back.

'We'd better leave,' said Tommy and shifted his gaze to Casper and smiled. 'Bye Casper. Hope you find a good home soon and a family that will give you the love you deserve.'

Hearing this made Iris cry too.

Sadly, the three friends turned around and walked slowly out of the yard.

CHAPTER 22

Tommy lifted his red bucket to reveal a sandcastle that took him just under a minute to build. 'Anyway Bella, as I was saying, I know this is the last thing you want to hear but there's a positive in what happened with Fredrick,' Tommy explained later that day as they relaxed in the afternoon sun at Indian Bay.

'And another good thing,' said Iris, sucking on a guava-flavoured popsicle. 'Your mum got to spend the rest of the day with you.'

Bella smiled under her broad-brimmed sun hat. Yes, she did. Bella was quiet for the rest of the day even though her friends tried to cheer her up. But nothing seemed to work. Bella felt so disappointed; she felt a tinge of sadness for Fredrick having to trick people into making money, and then little Casper. She could see his tiny face now. Poor Casper.

'It's so nice to see you smile,' said Tommy, building another sandcastle.

'Thanks, but for how long?' Bella rubbed sunblock along her arms although she sat in the shade.

'What do you mean for how long?' asked Iris, picking another popsicle from Isabel's cool box. 'Everything will be fine. Just stay positive and think of the wedding.'

Bella gazed out to the sea. 'The wedding with no clothes you mean? Time is ticking.'

The friends fell silent and stared ahead at the white yachts bobbing on the blue sea.

Private villas were visible in the distance as they backed onto a ribbon of golden sand. A group of noisy kids jumped off from rocks and dived headfirst into the depths of the cool water, while a group of grown-ups played Frisbee with bare feet in the sand.

Bella smiled at her mum who was busy dishing out the food she had cooked earlier. This warmed Bella's heart to know all the lovely food had not gone to waste.

Granny Sylta, adjusted the straps of her blue swimming costume and slid on a pair of goggles. 'I'm taking a dip, see you all later,' she said.

Kenneth had fallen asleep with his face under a newspaper, and the toddler was there too, but this time wearing only a nappy and a white sun hat.

Before going to the beach, Bella, Tommy, and Iris went to Troy's house to ask if he wanted to join them, but his dad had said he was not at home.

Bella's mum was full of smiles as she shaded her eyes from the sun and passed around avocado and cucumber sandwiches and the other food she had made. 'I'm so glad we managed to hang out today kids.' She looked around at everyone, as Tommy grabbed a handful of sandwiches.

Bella picked up her phone and pulled up the message from Fredrick again. She deleted it and threw the phone back into her beach bag.

Isabel stood up, dusting sand off her legs. 'I'm going to join Granny Sylta in the sea, I'll be a while.' Isabel waved and jogged across the hot sand towards where Granny Sylta was flapping her legs in the crispy white waves.

Tommy scoffed his sandwiches and raised a hand to the girls to grab their attention. 'We have no choice but to go back to Greiggs to see if we can spot the dog. To me it's obvious he lives in that area.' He looked at Bella, who gave no response and sat still staring at the ocean.

'It seems we have no choice now,' added Iris. 'What do you think, Bella?'

Bella shuffled up in her deck chair and looked ahead. 'I've decided I'm going to tell Mum everything. Today.'

Iris's mouth fell open and the popsicle juice dribbled down her chin.

Tommy almost choked on a mouth full of sandwiches.

'But we're so close,' pleaded Iris, spitting bits of popsicle juice everywhere. 'You can't give up now. You can't.'

'That's a brave move, but an honest one,' said Tommy, his mouth full of bread.

'Brave?' Bella sat up, her eyes blinking fast. 'This is not about being brave, we have no choice. The dog we're after has a keeper that speaks no English. The woman thinks we're trying to steal the dog. We got tricked into travelling all the way to Mesopotamia only to be presented with the wrong dog, and the dog with no name seems to have vanished into thin air. What else can possibly work against us?'

No one said another word until Tommy sat up.

'I've got it.' Tommy beamed a smile.

Iris sucked the juice from her popsicle really hard this time. 'This had better be good because I'm out of ideas.'

Bella blinked at him and folded her arms. 'So what are you suggesting?'

Tommy grabbed three more sandwiches from the platter and bit into one. 'Later, when we get back to the house, you'll see.' He grinned.

CHAPTER 23

Later that night after the family had fun in the games room, the three friends gathered in Tommy's bedroom for another meeting. This time Troy was invited over to discuss the next part of their plan and where he fitted in.

As promised, Tommy told Bella and Iris what he had in mind to win over the woman and gain access to the dog. They liked the idea very much.

'Troy, we need your help, it can work,' said Bella.

'Yes, this idea is genius. Please, you did say we should ask you if we needed help, right?' added Iris, as she closed the bedroom window again.

'We almost got the toy,' said Tommy. 'And she thought we were going to steal it.'

Troy looked at all three of them and giggled. He lifted his hands. 'I'm sorry, I didn't mean to laugh, it's just that you're all talking at one hundred miles per hour.'

Bella pursed her lips; this was no time for jokes.

Troy shuffled back and made himself more comfortable on the chair he sat on. 'So where do I come into all of this? How can I help you?' he rubbed his hands together.

Bella sat forward. 'The woman didn't understand a word of what we were saying, she blasted us in French, and we weren't able to communicate, so we didn't achieve our goal,' explained Bella.

'French?' said Troy.

'Yes,' said Iris. 'She was wearing a large St Lucian T-shirt with massive St Lucian earrings, so that explains the French I would imagine. And *you* speak French, Troy,' explained Iris.

Troy gave a shaky laugh. 'Well, I am learning.'

'Exactly,' Tommy added, 'And you said you love to try out your French on people you barely know, right?'

Troy gave an uncertain nod.

'So now that we have a rough idea of where the dog lives, we just have to go back there, find them and not lose them this time.' Tommy folded his arms with satisfaction.

'Yup, they vanished into thin air.' Iris shook her head.

Troy studied everyone's faces then happily said. 'I would be honoured to act as your translator.'

Bella and Iris high-fived Troy.

'Can you come with us tomorrow to retrace our steps to find them?' asked Bella.

Troy nodded enthusiastically. 'Let's leave after lunch. I have to help my dad finish painting the door frames in the morning. He likes to get his painting done as early as possible before the afternoon sun comes up. So knock for me at around 1 pm, and I'll be ready. The sooner we get this key, the better.'

The next day, as soon as the clock struck one, Bella and friends couldn't make it to Troy's house fast enough. They charged through the yard and hurtled up the steps almost tripping and falling through his front door.

But what they were greeted with was not what they were expecting.

'What on earth happened to you?' exclaimed Bella, taking in Troy's ragged appearance.

'You look like someone's dragged you through the wilderness,' said Iris.

Tommy also looked on with worry. 'Are you going to vomit?' he gazed around Troy's garden. 'Wanna bucket?'

Iris fanned her face in panic. 'Does this mean you can't come to Greiggs with us today?'

At first, Troy did not answer, instead, he pulled an odd face, and keeled over in pain.

Tommy grabbed an abandoned cardboard box and held it under Troy's mouth in case of a sudden sickly splurge.

Troy plopped himself down on a nearby stool holding the box close to his mouth that was dribbling with saliva as he spoke. 'It was my lunch,' he croaked. 'A homemade fish and green banana soup. It smelt a bit off. I thought it might have been the seasoning, however, my mum told me the fish had gone off and decided to leave it in the fridge to stop it from smelling up the house.'

Bella gasped. 'Good grief, poor you.'

Tommy and Iris shared worried glances.

Troy rubbed his belly and grimaced. 'I'm so sorry guys,' his voice was weak. 'I can't accompany you to find the dog. I was looking forward to it because you really need my help.'

Iris's knees knocked together and looked as if she may pass out.

Tommy's shoulders slumped slightly but he soon straightened himself again.

Bella felt the energy in her legs drain to her ankles. Was she able to stand up at all? Why oh, why, did things always appear to go pear-shaped whenever they were on the verge of moving one step forward? 'It's okay Troy,' said Bella. 'It's not your fault. There's no way you can leave home.' Bella blinked back her tears before anyone could notice them. 'I know I've said this when we were at the beach last, but I feel I must own up to Mum about this whole palaver. Things are going from bad to worse.'

'That's insane,' said Iris, taking a seat. 'What good would owning up do now? We're almost there.'

'Almost there? Still no key? Still no wedding frocks? And now, no translator?' said Tommy.

'Almost there?' Bella blurted, echoing Tommy. 'Can't you see everything is falling apart?' she gestured to Troy who was now heaving up his guts in the large box. The stinky fishy smell from his lunch filled the air.

Iris pinched her nose to block out the stench. 'I hear you, but if you tell Clara and Mum the key's missing, that won't solve anything. They'll just panic, especially Clara. We only have one day left to get the key before the wedding, the wedding is tomorrow, for heaven's sake, and all the clothes are still locked up in that thing that looks like a time machine.' Iris stamped her foot on the ground.

Then came a silence.

No one uttered a word and everyone turned to look at Troy who had flopped back into his chair with his eyes closed and mouth open.

'So what do you suggest?' Bella asked Iris. 'We have no exact whereabouts for the dog, only that it disappeared in the area of Greiggs, we don't know the house, its keeper speaks a language none of us know, and Google translator may as well speak Mandarin.'

Tommy wriggled his eyebrows again while Iris drummed her fingers against her chin in thought.

Bella huffed. 'I thought so, we're out of ideas, it's over.' She stood up quickly from her chair. 'I'm going back to Clara's. I'm going to tell Mum, Clara, and Granny Sylta the truth and end-all of this.' She turned to Troy. 'Get well soon Troy, so sorry this has happened to you and we'll check on you tomorrow.' Bella spun on her heel about to jog down the steps when a message pinged through on her phone.

HELLO THERE, THIS MESSAGE IS FOR BELLA, TOMMY, OR IRIS. I AM RESPONDING IN RELATION TO YOUR FLYER ABOUT THE DOG. WELL, I'M FOR SURE AND CERTAIN THAT DOG IS ONE OF MY NEIGHBOUR'S DOGS HERE IN GREIGGS. IF IT WEREN'T FOR THAT TOY SAUSAGE DOG IN ITS MOUTH, I WOULD HAVE NEVER TAKEN ANY NOTICE. SO THANKS TO THAT TOY, I BELIEVE THAT IS THE DOG YOU ARE LOOKING FOR, A POT CAKE DOG THAT'S ALWAYS WITH CELINE, ITS LADY DOG WALKER. PLEASE SEE THEIR ADDRESS BELOW. ALL THE BEST, THELMA. :)

CHAPTER 25

Whoever Thelma was; this time, she was spot on. The dog certainly did live at the address given in the text message.

In the front yard, the dog laid lazily next to two large plates of what seemed like leftovers.

Bella lifted her binoculars to her eyes once more and studied the movement of the blue house from behind a huge truck.

The house was not as large as Clara's but big enough, and it was surrounded by tall iron gates. Not much was happening apart from a loud TV that could be heard but there were no signs of the woman, who was now known as Celine.

Bella zoomed in on the toy sausage dog that was stretched out on the sandy ground a couple of feet away from the dog who seemed uninterested in its food.

'If we move to where the gate is, do you think it's possible to get the dog to pick up the toy and bring it over to us?' asked Tommy.

Iris gurgled with laughter. 'Tommy, I am surprised at your silly question.'

Bella lowered the binoculars from her eyes. 'It could be possible if we had something to lure the dog over with, but we have nothing.'

'That's what you think.' Tommy dived into his bag and pulled out something that was wrapped up in kitchen foil. He unwrapped it to reveal six shiny boiled eggs.

Iris laughed again. 'You're going to lure a dog over with eggs?'

Tommy didn't see the funny side and pulled out another packet of foil that had blocks of cheese, carrot sticks, chopped-up apples, slices of chicken, and sandwiches.

Bella's mouth fell open with amusement. 'Where did you get all that food?'

Tommy zipped up his rucksack. 'After it was clear that Troy couldn't make it, and when the message came through from Thelma, something urged me to pack some of the food that your Mum made for the beach picnic from the day before. I guessed if we managed to get close to the dog, we could lure it over with food.' Tommy also pulled out a carrier bag and took out three large hats and three pairs of sunglasses and gave the girls one of each.

Bella's eyebrows squished together. 'Okay, now I'm confused.'

'Me too,' said Iris.

Tommy slipped his hat and sunshades on. 'I figured we needed a disguise. In case we got close to the woman again, who knows, we may need to hide.'

Bella and Iris failed to hold back how impressed they were with Tommy's forward-thinking and planning.

They took the disguises and popped them in their bags.

'And seeing that he's out in the yard all by himself,' Tommy went on, 'Now's the time to try out my idea.'

'But what if he comes over to us at the gate and he leaves the toy sausage dog behind?' asked Bella.

'Chances are,' said Tommy. 'He'll bring the toy along. He's obsessed with it. Wherever he goes, so does the toy. Come on, let's make our way over.'

The girls followed Tommy as he led the way and crouched down beside a bush near the gate.

It was the furthest point from the house which meant it would be difficult to spot them if anyone came outside.

Tommy grabbed a handful of food, stuck his hand through the rail of the tall iron gate, and threw bits of egg and carrot sticks onto the ground.

The dog quickly lifted his head and stood on all fours.

'Oh my God,' squealed Bella. 'You've got his attention.'

The dog left its plate of half-eaten food, picked up the toy sausage dog, and trotted happily over to where Tommy had left the scraps of food.

'Aah! He picked up the toy!' yelled Iris.

'*Shhhhh*,' Bella told her. 'Keep it down. If Celine comes out and spots us, game over.'

In a high-pitched, but quiet voice, Tommy spoke to the dog. 'Hey boy.' He threw more bits of food near the gate, hoping this would bring the dog, and the toy, closer.

Finally, the dog dropped the toy sausage dog inches away from the food. Tommy stretched his hand through the railings.

'Go go go, get it now, Tommy,' Bella cheered quietly.

Tommy wriggled his fingers into the warm sand, stretching to get closer to the toy but still couldn't reach it.

Iris broke off a twig from the bush they hid behind. She poked it through the railings to try and edge the toy forward. But was one inch short of even touching the toy.

As the dog happily nibbled away at the apples, Tommy threw down some more food but closer to the gate.

A loud sneeze came from somewhere in the house and this forced Bella and her friends to look up sharply.

'Who's that?' whispered Bella.

'Sounded like a man's sneeze,' said Tommy, throwing down blocks of cheese, chicken bits, and cubes of apples even faster now.

Iris gasped. 'Oh no, look,' she pointed to the house.

Tommy and Bella looked up to see Celine slipping on a pair of shoes and a wide sun hat. Luckily, she didn't spot Bella and her friends as they continued to crouch in one corner.

They pulled back immediately.

The woman whistled to the dog and he turned his head. He picked up his toy and ran over to her leaving tiny scraps of food behind.

With defeat, Bella, Tommy, and Iris stared wide-eyed from the bush and heard the woman say something in French.

Attaching the lead around the dog's neck, they skipped through the yard, out of the iron gates, and down the street.

CHAPTER 26

'She's going on a tour?' squealed Tommy, from behind a guava tree.

'A tour bus?' echoed Iris, peering through the binoculars as she stood behind Tommy and Bella as they spied on the woman and dog hopping on a tour bus, unsure of what to do or where to hide next.

'So what now?' asked Iris. 'Shall we wait here until she returns seeing that we know where she lives? Surely we can't follow her on a tour bus, that certainly wasn't part of the plan, she'll recognise us,' Iris panicked.

Tommy rolled his eyes. 'Have you forgotten I've given you hats and glasses to disguise yourselves with? Put them on,' he ordered.

The girls' smiled embarrassingly and slipped out the accessories from their bags and popped them on.

'There.' Iris fixed her hat firmly on her head and so did Bella.

Tommy kept a watch on the tour bus as it filled up with tourists. 'I don't think we have a choice, Iris. We have to keep following and when an opportunity comes, we dive in, open the toy, grab the key, and voila.'

'A moment of opportunity like what though?' asked Iris again.

'Well, someone who has a dog will at some point always need to leave their dog alone, like pop into a shop, or for a toilet break.'

Bella clicked her fingers. 'Tommy, you're a genius.'

They watched as Celine climbed the steps up to the open-top deck and sat at the front with the dog next to her.

Bella, Tommy, and Iris ran up to the bus and boarded too.

They sat upstairs in the back row, ensuring their hats and sunglasses were covering their faces.

Tommy took a seat in front of the girls. 'Who would have thought we'd end up on a tour bus for this particular reason?' questioned Tommy.

Iris and Bella shrugged.

The bus, now filled up with tourists, roared into life and pulled away from the kerb.

It glided down the road passing low sweeping co-conut branches which tickled the tops of people's heads as the bus drove along passing more houses and shops.

The ride was smooth and, although the sun was at its hottest, the breeze from the open-top deck offered a refreshing coolness that Bella and her friends were grateful for.

A pretty woman with a large microphone stood up from one of the seats at the front and smiled at everyone. 'Hello all, welcome to the St Vincent and the Grenadines Island Tours, my name is Julie and I'm going to be your tour guide.' She pointed to a man who sat in a seat next to hers. 'And this here is my colleague, Lloyd who is here to help if you need anything.'

Lloyd smiled and nodded.

'Whoever has joined us has hopped on at the Greiggs route and today we are going to have fun,' said Julie.

Everyone cheered and whistled loudly.

Iris looked around amused. 'They're a joyful bunch aren't they?' she said to her friends, who nodded in response.

Julie continued, 'From here we're continuing clockwise around the island, starting with a drive past Argyle Beach, a cricket stadium tour at Arnos Vale, a drive-through Kingstown, and a visit to our biggest department store; Edwin D. Laynes, where you could perhaps buy some gifts. Then we'll be heading to the Botanical Gardens, from there up to Fort Charlotte, round to Buccament, Barrouallie, Walliabou Bay, cutting into Rose Bank and Richmond, and for the last part of this wonderful tour…' Julie took a deep breath. '…we'll be taking a nature trail, and finishing with a visit to our famous Trinity Falls.'

Everyone gasped this time while others *ooohed* with joy.

'Trinity Falls?' enquired Bella. 'Just how far away from home are we going? And where are these places?'

Tommy spun around to face the girls. 'It can't be all that far, it must be local. Remember St Vincent is not all that huge.'

Bella slid out her map from her rucksack to confirm. 'Oh, wow, look here.' She slid her finger along one side of the map. 'Tommy, I think you're wrong, St Vincent is not as small as you think. The tour route is going to cover the entire west side of the island which could take hours to get through.'

Tommy turned around again and grinned. 'The Leeward side I believe.'

'And how do you know?' asked Iris, lifting her large sun hat slightly so she could see his face.

'Because dear Iris, I know everything.'

Iris rolled her eyes.

Bella shoved the map back into her bag and took in the sights that whizzed past. 'I'm amazed at all the places the tour guide mentioned.'

'Same here, it sounds so exciting, like we're going on a big Caribbean adventure.' Iris popped a sweet in her mouth. 'But let's not forget the reason why we're on this bus in the first place.'

The three friends shifted their gaze to the front of the bus and kept their eyes firmly on Celine ... and their furry friend.

CHAPTER 27

Two hours into the tour, Bella, Tommy, and Iris had seen an eyeful of St Vincent and a glimpse of Caribbean life, the mountainous landscapes, and the rich history.

Bella was bursting with excitement with all she had learned and couldn't wait to return to school in September to tell her friends and her teacher, Mrs Mardell, what she had discovered.

Fancy that? Bella thought as she wrote in her reporter's notebook. Fort Charlotte was not only named after Queen Charlotte, but it was the only Fort she had heard of that was not built to protect the island from naval attack, but instead, to protect it from people already on the island who were known as the Caribs.

As the tour bus continued to zoom through more leafy villages, Bella also discovered who Chief Joseph Chatoyer was, the man in the large portrait hanging on Clara's dining room wall.

According to what Julie said, Joseph had led Britain into war after they had tried to take over the island. Joseph had hoped to remove the British for good and how the battle that was fought was the scariest of its kind. Bella stopped writing and began to chew her pen. She wondered if Joseph and the Caribs had to defend themselves from Pirates too?

As promised, after leaving Fort Charlotte, twenty minutes later the tour bus arrived at the Botanical Gardens.

At the entrance stood a beautiful sign in the shape of an arch.

Bella looked up and smiled when she saw it and took a photograph. The words on the arch read: "*The Botanical Gardens, founded in 1765*". How awesome was that? Bella wondered if the garden was always that huge when it started back then, or at one time was it the size of someone's back garden? And with each year it just grew and grew to what it was now?

She considered for a moment and scribbled her thoughts into her notebook.

Bella joined her friends and played in the gardens, smelt the flowers, ran underneath leafy arches, read another sign about St Vincent's famous parrot, and took pictures in front of a green and white wishing well with lily leaves and water in the centre.

Although having so much fun, Bella and her friends kept a firm eye on Celine and the dog in case she took a toilet break.

'It's been just over two hours, and she still ain't gone toilet?' Complained Tommy, slipping his sun-shades up to the bridge of his sun-baked nose.

'Don't worry,' said Iris, fixing her large hat on her head. 'Our time will come. She must have to take a toilet break at some point.'

The tour guide signalled for everyone to leave the beautiful gardens and make their way back to the bus when Bella noticed Celine was chatting to Lloyd, the other tour guide.

As the dog sniffed out all the flowers, Lloyd nodded and pointed towards a building marked "toilets."

'Bingo!' squealed Bella. 'You're right Tommy, 'Celine's finally having a toilet break.'

The kids quickly back-tracked through the tour party who were still making their way to the bus in the opposite direction.

They hid behind a couple of rose bushes and fixed their eyes on Celine.

'Wait until she goes in,' instructed Tommy. 'Bella, you run around the side near the toilet doors. When she goes in, give the dog this.' Tommy pulled out the same piece of tin foil from his bag and gave it to Bella. 'It's peanut butter sandwiches.'

Iris snorted a laugh.

'Walk up to the dog,' said Tommy. 'Drop it on the grass, when the dog drops the toy to eat the sandwich, pick it up and leg it out of there, got it?'

Bella nodded so fast she thought her head was going to snap off. She took the food from Tommy and headed in the direction he told her to.

Iris stayed with Tommy behind the rose bush as they waited for Celine to go inside.

Finally reaching the building, Celine escorted the dog to a nearby coconut tree and tied the lead around the trunk.

Bella crouched down even further and peeped through her binoculars between the flowers. Her hands were slick with sweat.

Celine walked up to a door that had the words "Ladies Toilet" written above it. She pushed it open and went inside.

Great, thought Bella and raised a fist to Tommy and Iris who was on the other side.

Itching to make her move, Bella stood up preparing to leap out of the bush, but as she lifted one foot to jump, the toilet door swung open and Celine came out.

Bella froze. Go back inside! She screamed to herself. What was Celine doing?

The woman strolled up to the dog, unhooked the lead from the tree trunk, and took the dog back inside, closing the toilet door.

'Why?' Bella wanted to scream. She spied across the clearing towards where Tommy and Iris were and saw them stamping angrily on the grass.

Suddenly, the tour bus gave three big honks to alert whoever was still not on the bus to board quickly.

With one hand on her large hat, Bella scrambled through a flurry of rose bushes to meet her friends and they scarpered onto the bus. The kids took their seats once more and everyone waited for Celine and the dog to return.

CHAPTER 28

Three hours later they passed a monument, a plantation house, and a village where the residents of the Carib descendants could still be found.

Tommy took many photos of buildings and spoke enthusiastically about the architecture, while Iris drew churches, coconut fields and boats they had passed.

The sun shone brightly, the tour party was in high spirits and Celine and the dog were also still having a good time.

Julie stood up and turned to face everyone. 'Ladies and gentlemen, we have now reached the last leg of this amazing Caribbean adventure tour and welcome you to Richmond Village!' she bellowed into the microphone and stretched out one arm to emphasise the welcome.

Everyone filed into a single line, made their way down the stairs and off the bus. They gathered into large groups on the grass and shaded under trees.

Bella, Tommy, and Iris, although still in disguise held back from Celine, but she appeared to be chatting away on her phone.

Richmond village was beautiful. There were more colourful houses and the pace of life was more relaxing compared to town.

Locals played Soca music from their radios and ate roasted breadfruit with chicken on paper plates, while others glugged down bottles of Juicy in the evening sun.

Julie beckoned for everyone's attention by raising her hand. 'For those who wish to do the bird spotting tour, please gather over on the left and join Lloyd. And for those who prefer to join me and take part in the nature trail, zip-lining, and Trinity Falls activity, stand over to the right.' she smiled. 'Once you've chosen which tour to follow, we'll meet back here in three hours.'

Everyone nodded and smiled.

Iris put a hand to her chest in horror. 'Did she say zip-lining?'

'I think you heard right,' said Bella, adjusting the large hat on her head. She sat on the grass and rubbed her neck with worry. 'I don't like heights.'

'Me too,' said Iris. 'I can't go through another Ferris wheel fiasco.'

Tommy threw his head back with laughter. 'Hang on a minute Iris, weren't you excited to get on a plane

BELLA'S BIG CARIBBEAN ADVENTURE

to fly out here? And told Bella how being on a plane is okay because you're safe inside?' he giggled.

Iris opened her mouth and said nothing.

Bella shuddered. 'Well, zip-lining is out of the question for me.'

Tommy tapped Bella on the shoulder with a grin. 'Sure, but if Celine and our furry friend decide to go zip-lining, what are you going to do?'

'What do you mean?' Bella's heart fluttered. 'I won't join in, simple.'

Iris nodded fast. 'Me neither.'

'And besides,' Bella went on. 'Who would take a dog zip-lining anyway? It's impossible.'

'Wanna bet?' replied Tommy, pointing towards Celine who had joined everyone on the right.

'Oh my God,' said Bella. 'She wants to do the zip-lining?'

Iris covered her eyes with her hands.

'But how is she going to do that? Surely the dog can't zip-line by itself,' panicked Bella.

'That's what I was thinking,' chimed in Iris. 'There's no way the dog can hold on with its paws.'

'Come on girls.' Tommy threw his hands in the air. 'Let's not waste time on whether the dog can zip-line or not, I couldn't care less if it knew how to knit scarves. We need to join everyone on the right to be in with a chance for another opportunity. Let's go.'

They ran over to join the group and stood at the back to keep out of Celine's view although still in disguise.

As both parties broke off into opposite directions, Bella and her friends shuffled along in an orderly fashion while keeping a firm eye on the dog.

CHAPTER 29

One hour later, the Trinity Falls tour party found themselves in thick tropical woodland. It was magical, it smelt delightful, it sparkled, and a cacophony of interesting noises from birds and other wildlife played out over the towering stumps of banana trees like an animal orchestra.

Narrow paths, some of them no wider than a ribbon, melted into leafy trails. Some of the trails dipped so low it became as dark as night. Whereas other paths climbed so high it was almost like walking skyward.

They continued to follow the path that brought them out into a clearing and a fairytale-style humpedback bridge welcomed them.

The bridge arched over trickles of crystal clear flowing water that was so clean it looked good enough to drink.

'Oh look!' cried out one man. 'A stream!'

A group of tourists galloped all the way to the edge of the stream, and one by one they unscrewed the caps off their bottles and began to fill them up and drink the cool water. As fast as they filled, they drank it all down.

Bella and friends were in awe; it was like nothing they had ever seen.

'Only now do I feel like a pirate,' said Tommy to the others.

They joined everyone and filled up their bottles too.

Tommy glugged back mouthfuls.

'I never would have predicted today would have gone like this,' said Bella, pouring cool water over her face and neck.

'Neither would I,' replied Iris. 'We were only meant to go to Greiggs, but look where we've ended up.'

Celine and the dog were over on the far side filling up bottles too. The dog dipped its mouth into the stream and drank happily while wagging its tail.

A group of girls wearing baggy T-shirts with Grenada splashed across the front, tip-toed into the cool water, and waded in until the water reached their waists.

Julie congratulated everyone on completing the nature trail part of the tour with no hiccups.

She instructed everyone to follow her up a long wooden man-made staircase that creaked and swayed with every step.

Iris trembled and held on tight while Tommy powered on ahead, leaving Bella to pick her way through with caution.

Finally, they reached the top of the staircase where everyone had gathered.

'Now, this is where the fun starts,' said Julie, stretching out her arm to reveal a 200 meter-long zip line that disappeared into a rich green thicket of a tropical forest way down below.

Iris trembled and Tommy put an arm around her.

'Don't worry Iris,' said Tommy. 'As soon as the tour guide mentioned the zip-line part, I Googled whether it was dangerous, and according to what I read, apart from getting an adrenaline rush,' he paused to laugh. 'Only twelve percent of zip-line injuries have resulted in fractures or other injuries that required urgent medical attention. It also mentioned how it is ranked as dangerous as rock climbing,' he said proudly.

Iris clenched her fists and turned to face him. 'Tommy?'

'Yes?' He grinned.

'Shut. Up.'

Everyone began to pass helmets around and each popped one on their head.

One of the zip-line team attached a weird vest to Celine's body.

Bella narrowed her eyes at Celine. 'What the ...'

Tommy laughed. 'That odd vest is to hold the dog in as she glides down the zip-line.'

Bella shook her head. 'You learn something new every day.'

One by one, everyone braced themselves to take a turn.

A woman wearing a floral jumpsuit took at least fifteen minutes to let go of the platform handles. She closed her eyes, released a glass-shattering scream, and descended, disappearing into a blanket of swaying palm treetops spread out below.

Celine and the dog were next and like a pro, she allowed herself to freely glide downwards.

Tommy went next, then Bella and surprisingly Iris, who of course needed a little push.

As soon as all three reached the bottom, Tommy and Bella gave Iris a pat on the back for trying to face her fear. Moments after, they scanned the area for Celine. They spotted her crouching down behind a very large bush and the dog a few feet away.

'Oh blast,' said Bella, she's gone to the toilet again, but still no chance of getting near that dog.'

Tommy shook his head. 'Just give it time. There has to be at least a minute where she's not around the dog. Just remember to keep looking for those opportunities.'

Bella folded her arms. 'My patience is wearing thin.'

'Well it can't,' he said. 'We've come so far, not only in miles but into this investigation. The wedding is tomorrow,' Tommy reminded them.

Iris blew out her cheeks and gazed around. 'Just how far away from home are we anyway?'

'Tommy shrugged and looked up to the late evening sky that was the colour of burnt orange. 'I don't know, but I'd imagine we're really far. It's been hours since we left home.'

CHAPTER 30

Everyone, including Bella, Tommy, and Iris could sense that Trinity Falls was close by. The tiny fresh cool water stream had now turned into a full-flowing river. Flashes of blue sky peeped in between a canopy of swaying leaves to reveal insects darting to and fro.

The air was thick with a sweet scent of mango and banana, and the rippling sound of water could be heard everywhere.

The tour party seemed cheery and everyone chatted merrily as they trampled leaves and pointed out birds that swooped and flitted all around them.

Bella's camera snapped away at nearly every colourful thing she passed and scribbled more notes in her notebook when her phone buzzed. She took out her phone and realised her mum had called twice with a message:

Hi Bella, just texting to see if the three of you are okay. I assume you are with Troy again. Just let me know how you're doing and send me back a message. Thanks. Mum. X

Bella quickly texted her mum back and told her all was good and she needn't worry. She put her phone and notebook away and continued with the nature trail.

The river rolled alongside them as it snaked through the forest when suddenly a group of loose paddle boats bobbed close to the riverside.

Next to it was a tiny hut with the words "River Police" marked up in white letters.

Julie took her usual position in front of the group. 'How's everyone doing?' she asked in a joyful tone.

Everyone cheered with raised fists.

Celine was over on the far side taking pictures of the river while the dog sniffed among the flower beds.

'This is the final part of the nature trail and now we're going to the best part … Trinity Falls. We'll be making our way along the river and when we get there you'll be able to bathe in the famous hot springs that many tourists travel the world to experience.'

'Wow!' said a lady in a bright pink swimming suit.

'Can't wait!' said a man wearing an England T-shirt.

'So please follow me.' Julie strode off and everyone followed.

Bella glanced behind her and noticed Celine appeared to be panicked as if she was looking for something. Oh dear, she wondered what was wrong. 'Guys, stop,' Bella called to her friends. 'Look over there.' She pointed to Celine who was now crying.

Tommy ran up to the tour guide. 'A member of our group seems to be in a bit of trouble.'

Julie stopped and looked over her shoulder. 'Wait everyone!' She made her way over to Celine with Bella, Tommy, and Iris tottering behind, along with a few others.

'What's happened?' asked Julie.

'Mon chien, oh non, s'il vous plaît, je ne peux pas trouver mon chien. Aidez-moi!' sobbed Celine.

Julie placed a hand to her heart. 'I'm so sorry, I don't understand French.' She looked around for help and spotted Lloyd on the far side of the forest. 'Lloyd!' she called out, but he was knee-deep in tropical woodland and too busy trying to find the dog to even hear her.

Celine continued to sob. 'Je ne peux pas perdre mon bébé, je ne veux pas qu'elle meure. Oh s'il vous plait, non!'

Bella exchanged hopeless glances with her friends wishing Troy was with them.

One man stepped forward. 'I understand French. She said she lost her dog and she can't lose her baby.'

Bella gasped. 'Oh my God, the dog is lost? And it's somewhere out here on its own?' she gazed around in wonder.

Tommy stepped forward now. 'Don't worry, we'll help you find it, won't we girls?' he gave his friends a knowing look that translated as, "here's our opportunity".

Bella and Iris nodded quickly.

The man who understood French looked on with concern. 'I'll ask her what the dog's name is, that should make it easier to locate the dog.'

Iris jigged excitedly on her feet and quietly said to her friends. 'Finally, we're going to know the name of the dog, with no name.'

In French, the man asked Celine for the dog's name, but seconds after, Celine fainted.

CHAPTER 31

With Celine passed out and flat on her back, and with the man who understood French fanning Celine's face with a huge banana leaf, Julie instructed everyone to scurry around the forest.

The dog had to be found as soon as possible before sunset, or the chances of finding their way out of the forest in complete darkness would be impossible.

This motivated everyone to immediately scatter themselves across the tropical woodland; parting bushes and whistling and yelling for the dog.

Bella, Tommy, and Iris dashed into the thick of the forest among the tall grasses and trees, and called out to the dog that still had no name, so they called out the word, "dog."

Bella looked back and spotted Tommy by the river and Iris searching along a trail overflowing with tropical plants and blooms.

'Who would have guessed the dog would separate itself now instead of during a toilet break,' Bella muttered under her breath.

Shouts from other people could be heard as the search continued.

How worrying is this to lose a dog around here. Bella understood the panic; if night fell and there was still no sign of it, she could imagine how scary this forest would look at night with no lights. Poor dog.

A couple of paddle boats with people inside playing loud music sailed past, oblivious to the chaos on the bankside as they danced away.

Something caught Bella's eye that moved behind a tree that was next to the group of paddle boats. The tree had a huge trunk and the branches overhung at almost height level.

She tip-toed up to the tree and stood on the bankside. Leaning around the trunk she saw the dog. She wanted to squeal and alert everyone, but the dog was happily drinking the river water and the sausage dog was beside him on the grass.

The dog was in a world of its own, lapping up the cool water like apple juice. This was Bella's chance. The chance she had been waiting for.

Ever so gently, Bella tiptoed nearer, and in a soft voice, she said, 'Now, now, there's a good boy. Let me see your toy, what a lovely toy you have there.' She stooped to pick it up but the dog growled. He sunk his teeth into the toy and refused to let go.

Bella held onto the sausage dog too and tightened her grip but the dog held on.

They continued to pull this way and that, like a game of tug of war until Bella yanked the toy so hard it flew backward and landed in one of the paddle boats which began to drift slowly along the bank.

The dog dashed away to the riverside and jumped into the boat when someone screamed out from behind her.

'*Yoooooou!*'

Bella whipped round to find Celine up on her feet, shaking with anger, and with a face like thunder.

Chapter 32

Celine's scream forced members of the entire party who were now spread out throughout the forest to stop and look around.

'What's going on?' said one of the girls wearing the Grenada T-Shirt.

'I think it's a woman,' said a man wearing a string vest.

Bella noticed when Tommy and Iris looked around sharply too, and the horror on their faces when they realised Celine had seen through her disguise.

Holding onto their large hats, Tommy and Iris rushed over.

'Bella, are you okay?' asked Tommy.

'I found the dog, and the toy was on the ground so I moved in to grab it but he wouldn't let go.'

'Where's the dog now?' asked Iris.

Bella pointed to the boat that had slowly drifted away from the shore and downstream. 'He's in that boat!'

'But how are we going to get the dog now?' asked Iris.

Tommy pointed to the cluster of paddle boats on the side. 'Quick, let's jump in one and follow.'

Iris widened her eyes. 'You mean to follow the dog?'

Bella pushed past Iris and got into the boat. 'Of course, what else? Tommy and Iris, you two row, and I'll keep watch.'

Iris and Tommy grabbed a paddle on the port and starboard of the boat while Bella sat in the stern and took on the position of a Coxswain.

The boat with the dog in it was now about twenty feet ahead of them and squeals and shouts from the tourists rang out into the evening air as word got around that the dog had been located.

Bella spotted Celine raising her fists while the other tourists shouted words. Bella cocked her ear trying to listen but all she heard was the word, "ball". Hmm, what did they mean?

Tommy and Iris paddled fiercely but made little headway. She thought back to the last Olympics in 2016 when she watched a boating race with her dad. She must have been only five, but she remembered some of the things the men shouted. Now, what were they?

'Bella,' said Tommy, interrupting her thoughts. 'Are we getting closer?'

Bella's heart sank a little. The dog was getting further and further away. She willed herself to remember, then suddenly she did. 'Okay, listen, I'm going to chant some words to help speed up this boat, when I say them, row your heart out, got it?'

Tommy and Iris nodded.

'Okay: Legs! Drive! Go! and Push! Legs! Drive! Go! and Push!' Bella repeated this over and over again and noticed the boat gained a little speed.

She said it faster and faster, louder and louder.

The dog's boat was drawing nearer which brought a bit of hope. We're finally going to get this key!

Still, with the toy in his mouth, the dog was sitting happily in the boat.

'We've nearly got him, come on guys!' said Bella, 'Move it! Move it!'

Sweat poured off Iris as she pushed and pulled the oar. 'We must get the key, we must get the key,' she chanted.

Tommy chose not to chant anything and focused on the calls that Bella gave to motivate him.

'Look! We're so close now!' Bella pointed.

Tommy and Iris spun around to find their boat was almost touching the stern of the other.

'Yes! We did it!' Tommy punched the air.

Screams were heard from the bankside as the flurry of tourists had ran downstream to cheer them on.

My goodness, thought Bella, this was like an Olympic boat race for real.

The tour guide waved her hands in the air and shouted a string of words that were difficult to hear over the noise.

Bella still didn't understand what Julie meant by the word "ball". She ignored the screams and told her friends to quickly hop into the dog's boat.

Tommy stepped into the other boat first and then Iris.

'Right Tommy,' said Bella. 'Take out the food you've got wrapped in foil, put it on the floor for the dog to eat so we can grab his toy.'

Tommy fought to open his rucksack, took out the food, and spread it all over the floor of the boat.

First, the dog sniffed out the chicken bits, cheese and apples then dropped the sausage dog on the floor and began to eat.

Bella swiped up the toy and they cheered and hugged each other.

'Yeah! We did it! At last!' said Bella.

'Let's now row back to shore to meet the others,' said Iris.

Tommy nodded. 'Yes, but before we do that, take the key out of the toy before we hand the dog back to Celine.'

'Good idea,' laughed Bella. She tipped the sausage dog upside down and felt a few things inside. 'I can feel something.' She shook it again but it was stuck. She tried to squeeze it when one of the things tipped into her hand. She frowned.

'What is it, Bella?' Iris said in a shaky voice, as the boat gently picked up speed again.

'It's not the key, it's a pencil.'

'What do you mean a pencil?' asked Iris.

'Try again,' said Tommy.

She squeezed it again and this time a red button fell out, then an earring, a cornflake, and a baby's tooth. She shook it again and it was completely empty. 'There's nothing more inside.' Bella cried out. 'It must have slipped out somewhere.'

'But there's no way it could have slipped out,' said Tommy. 'The hole is smaller than the key itself.'

'So how do you think these other things got inside? They too are bigger than the hole,' said Bella.

'But I remember the day the toddler stuffed the key in the toy, he forced it in. Chances of it falling out are slim,' suggested Tommy. 'Here, let me try.' He grabbed the toy off Bella, shook it madly, swung it around in a circle, but nothing else fell out.

Iris covered her face with her hands. 'What do we do now?'

Tommy gazed out to the river bank where everyone still gathered, talking in raised voices. 'Hurry, let's paddle back to shore.'

Iris grabbed an oar, Tommy did the same and began to steer the boat around.

They slowly pushed through the waves and picked up a little speed.

'Is it me or does the boat seem more difficult to steer this time?' Tommy asked Iris.

'Definitely,' she groaned.

Everyone on the bankside appeared to be going out of their minds, yelling, screaming and jumping up and down, and waving their arms in the air.

'Why is everyone acting so weird? We're only in a paddleboat,' said Iris.

The boat picked up more speed and the breeze danced off the river.

Tommy shrugged. 'Beats me. We saved the dog and hopefully, Celine will forgive us now our cover is blown.' Tommy smiled at the dog as it laid quietly by Bella's feet.'

Bella chose not to be a Coxswain this time around, there was no need to race back to shore.

Again, the screams from the tourists grew louder and louder when suddenly the boat moved at a much faster pace until Tommy and Iris were now struggling to keep the boat moving in one direction.

'What's happening?' panicked Iris. 'Why has the boat suddenly gotten a mind of its own?'

'I'm not sure,' said Tommy.

'Try to steer the boat over to the shore,' instructed Bella.

They rowed with all their might but it was no use. The boat tossed this way and that, it moved even faster now and Tommy stood up. He tried to balance himself by stretching his arms out. As the boat sailed fast, he reached up to grab a few overhanging branches to help slow the speed of the boat.

He grabbed hold of one but it snapped off in his hand. He wobbled and just about stopped himself from falling overboard.

Iris covered her eyes again and squealed.

'Tommy, get down!' Bella pleaded. 'Now! Before something bad happens, please.'

Tommy ignored Bella and tried to grab another branch. Again he missed and wobbled.

The dog sensed trouble. He stood up, picked his toy, and leaped out of the boat. Diving headfirst into the river, the dog swam its way to shore.

'Oh no, the dog has left us!' screamed Iris.

The tour party on the bankside continued to shout at the tops of their voices and were now pointing to something in the distance.

'They're pointing at something, but I don't know what.' Iris picked up an oar once more to try and guide the boat.

The dog headed straight into the arms of Celine. She hugged him and burst into more tears.

'What's that noise?' Iris shielded her eyes from the evening sun.

'What noise?' asked Bella, peering around.

'That rumbling sound,' replied Iris.

Tommy furrowed his brow. 'Yes, I can hear it too, what is it?'

All three squinted as they gazed into the distance and their eyes popped with horror.

'No, no, no, no.' Bella's legs wobbled.

Tommy sat down in disbelief. 'That can't be what I think it is.'

'Yes, it is what you think it is,' cried Iris. 'It's a waterfall. *Heeeeeeelp!*'

CHAPTER 33

Only then did Bella realise why everyone was acting weird, and what the tour guide lady was shouting was not "ball", it was fall, Trinity Falls.

'We're done for now, finished,' Iris's voice trembled as she cried out.

Tommy, for the first time, was speechless.

'Tommy?' Bella shook him. 'Tommy?' he didn't answer and was frozen to the spot.

Bella felt the blood drain from her face.

Iris screamed as the boat zoomed down the river at breakneck speed as though it were a speed boat going at fifty miles per hour. 'This is not a big Caribbean adventure,' Iris roared, face as red as a tomato. 'This is one big Caribbean disaster! And we're gonna die!'

Bella thought of her mum. Imagine, all this because she never listened to her mum who simply told her she was not allowed to look at a bunch of silly dresses. Now she may not even live to wear the dress.

Bella stood up slowly, legs astride to keep her balance, and tried to do what Tommy did. She reached out to grab over-hanging branches but they were out of reach. She tried with all her might but it was no use, she was not as tall as Tommy.

Suddenly Tommy rose to his feet and lifted one of the oars above his head, allowing it to knock along the branches.

Bella's skin tingled with fear when she saw Tommy on his feet. 'What are you doing, Tommy? Put the oar down!' her voice was a pitch higher than normal.

'I'm trying to slow the flow of the boat by jamming the oar up into the branches,' he explained.

The oar made a deafening clattering sound as it brushed along the branches and this made a tiny bit of difference to the speed.

'Well done Tommy!' cried out Iris. 'I think it's working.'

Bella's eyes shifted to Trinity Falls and it roared like a thousand thunderstorms.

Tommy growled like a warrior as he fought to jam the paddle high up into the branches for a final attempt to slow the boat. When finally it did just that, it got stuck, however, the force of the current threw him sideways. He lost balance, slipped backward and fell overboard, head first, into the river.

'TOMMMMY!'

CHAPTER 34

The top of Tommy's head bobbed up and down beneath the current as the girls sailed and spun away clinging to the insides of the boat.

The bankside was now heaving with more tourists from other tour buses as they joined forces to witness the cause of the chaos. So many people had gathered there that Bella struggled to spot the individuals from her own tour party.

Iris shivered like a wet dog and cried out for her mum. 'Mummy!'

Bella scanned the river to see if she could spot Tommy. He had somehow managed to cling onto a few low-hanging branches. 'Tommy's safe! Now we need to get off the boat before it reaches the waterfall!'

Iris, now soaked, stuck her fingers in her ears and nodded, however, Bella knew Iris would never jump.

With about 200 yards left before they hit the fall, Bella pulled out the one remaining paddle from the boat and swiped at anything in their path: branches, rocks, but it was no use, she was too short and barely touched the tips of the branches. The rocks forced the paddle to bounce back, jerking Bella sideways.

'Iris, we need to jump.'

Iris shook her head. 'No, never.'

'But we're heading for Trinity Falls!' shouted Bella.

'And if we jump off, we'll get swallowed by the current.'

The sprays from the river felt more like beats and somehow the tourists, running along the bank, managed to catch up with them.

Bella stared ahead and spotted one last low-hanging branch they could grab onto. 'Iris, stand up. We have one more chance. We need to grab onto that branch as we sail past, or over Trinity Falls we go. Now come on.'

Iris stood up and spotted the branch that stood out like a long wrist with skeletal fingers. It looked alive as it swayed with the waves as if instructing them to hurry up. Iris took the deepest breath she had ever taken in her life. 'Okay let's go.'

The girls shifted and positioned themselves in line with the tree as they drew nearer. They stretched out their arms, preparing to grab it.

Iris kept her eyes firmly on the branch. 'Here goes.'

As they approached it, a siren blared out in the distance.

Iris saw a boat with a siren on top and a sign across its front which read "River Police".

With only twenty yards to go, Bella noticed Iris's chin and lips were trembling with fear, and Bella's heart thrashed against her chest.

'We can do it! We can!' shouted Bella, with her arms stretched out in front of her. 'Get ready!'

'I am Bella, I am!' yelled Iris.

The River Police sped towards them as more crowds gathered in shock.

Bella took another deep breath and gave Iris one last glance. 'Okay Iris, you ready.'

'Yes!'

'Okay. One … two … three … grab the branch Iris! Graaaab it!'

CHAPTER 35

'That was great thinking young lady,' the Chief of River Police said to Bella as he finished taking her report. 'If it weren't for that branch, and your quick thinking, you may not be standing here, so well done, you're a little hero,' he told her.

Bella didn't feel like a hero at all. She felt guilty about many things tonight, and one of them was not being home on time and getting a good night's sleep for Clara's wedding tomorrow instead of being at the opposite end of the island in wet clothes and soggy socks.

Tommy sat on a folding chair provided by the River Police and sipped on a large cup of tea with a blanket wrapped around him.

Iris was a few yards away and for the last thirty minutes she chatted to another member of the rescue team.

What could she be talking about? Wondered Bella.

'What on earth made you jump into a paddleboat? Those currents are strong,' asked the officer.

Bella could barely keep her tired eyes open. 'It's a long story, but it involves a dog.'

The officer raised an eyebrow and smiled. 'Oh, I know those ones. You love your dog, but be careful not to risk your life like that again. Rescuing a dog that's fallen in a river is a job for experienced River Police, not a kid.'

Bella nodded. 'You're right, but you don't understand, the dog isn't my pet he belongs to—'

'It's okay, it's getting late and we have a duty to take you, kids, home.'

Bella's head flipped up. 'Home?'

'Yes, don't you want to go home?' He laughed.

Bella grinned uncomfortably. 'I want to go home, it's just…' What would her mum think if she saw them rolling up the drive in a police car?

'It's just what?' he asked.

'Oh, nothing.'

He put his cap on his head. 'I'm going to prepare the minibus with more blankets for you and your friends and we'll get you home.' He smiled and walked off in the direction of where the minibus was parked.

'Bella!' Julie ran up to Bella, and out of breath. 'I'm so glad you're all alive, I prayed that you'd make it.'

'Thank you,' said Bella. 'And we're sorry for ruining the last part of your amazing tour. I hope you don't get into trouble.'

She laughed and hugged Bella. 'Don't you worry about me I'm just glad everything turned out alright.'

Bella's mind flitted to the dog. 'Is the dog okay? Where is he?'

'He's gone home with his owner, they left about an hour ago with everyone else who was on the tour. I stayed behind to ensure everything was good with you guys.'

Bella smiled. 'Thank you. Too bad we never got to experience the hot springs near the falls.'

'I think that's the least of your worries.'

Bella agreed. It sure was. What was she going to tell her mum now?

Julie hugged Bella once more and headed towards the tour bus.

The Chief of Police motioned the kids to take their seats in the minibus and they climbed in one by one.

Tommy sat opposite the girls and pulled his blanket around him. 'Listen, girls, when we arrive back to Cane Garden, we've got to sneak into the house, get showered, then into bed, and try to get as much sleep before the wedding tomorrow.'

'What wedding?' Bella sipped her tea. 'A wedding with no clothes locked up in that time-capsule-of-a-wardrobe?'

Tommy pursed his lips.

167

'Well here's what I think we should do,' said Iris, shifting round. 'Forget sneaking into the house, let's get the police to drop us a few doors away from Clara's, then we sneak up the garden path, up the stairs, get showered and into bed,' said Iris.

Tommy grinned and nodded.

'That's a good idea,' complimented Bella, 'Mum and everyone else will never know. Like we never left.'

The minibus drove off and Bella turned one last time. She looked at the river when the driver turned up the radio.

"Good evening, and welcome to hot 97 SVG news. A breaking news story has just come in.

Two hours ago the St Vincent River Police were called to an incident that took place at Trinity Falls.

Three children who were on the last leg of the Big Caribbean Adventure Island Tour ran into trouble when an eyewitness said the kids who boarded a paddleboat drifted downstream after trying to rescue their pet dog.

One of the children, a boy, fell into the river which left him clinging to a tree, leaving two girls behind.

The emergency River Police services rushed to the scene at about 7.40 pm. The River Police used an extension ladder to rescue the two girls, and the boy, who was eventually brought to safety.

The three children will be reunited with their families: Bella Matthews, Iris O'Connell, and Tommy Smith, who reside in England are currently visiting St Vincent for a friend's wedding. And now for other news.

CHAPTER 36

'How was I supposed to know our business would have ended up all over Hot 97 SVG News?' complained a terrified Iris to a furious Bella and a shocked Tommy, as they were summoned to Clara's huge marble kitchen for the ear-bashing of their lives.

With their hair wet, clothes still damp, and squelching shoes, their feet squeaked like mice with every step as they left muddy footprints and puddles of water down the hall.

Apparently, Iris admitted she had a lovely chat and a cup of tea with one of the river officers, and revealed their names, where they were from, and why they were on the island.

Iris sobbed into a hanky as her legs wobbled with fear. 'We're all gonna die, for sure. Isabel is gonna kill us.' She blew her nose and looked at Tommy. 'Me and my big mouth. Tommy, help me. I'm so scared that Isabel will—'

'Zip it, Iris. Just, Zip it,' snapped Bella, who reached the kitchen door first and pushed it open ever so gently.

She peeped in to find her mum, Granny Sylta, and Clara sitting on bar stools with their arms folded and no peak of a smile. They looked like courtroom judges waiting to pass a sentence.

With their heads bowed, the kids trembled as they did the walk of shame and squeaked their way in, across the kitchen, passed the dining area, and stood in front of the three grown-ups.

Isabel's eyes flashed with anger as she stared at them. 'I trusted you, Bella. Every. Single. Word. How dare you? What on earth were you thinking of?'

Bella turned to look at her friends who dared not look sideways.

'What were you doing taking a tour bus all the way to Trinity Falls? You could have died, all three of you. I didn't believe it when the river police rang to tell me what had happened. But then Clara confirmed it when she heard it on the radio.' Isabel rubbed her temples. 'Everyone in the neighbourhood, no actually, on the island is talking about it. And all of this on the eve of Clara's wedding.'

No one spoke. There was not a sound apart from the chirps from the crickets outside.

'This beautiful holiday could have ended in tragedy. Tommy's parents would have been devastated,

Iris's too, and I would have gotten into so much trouble because I would have been held responsible.' She stared at Iris and Tommy, then back at Bella again. 'You told me you were going to stay local and visit your friend next door. You never told me you had planned to go on a tour bus all the way to the top of the island. That could have been something we all could have done together.' Isabel slid off the breakfast stool and stood in front of the children; her eyes scanned Bella's face again. 'Why Bella? Why?'

Bella's eyes filled with tears and she began to cry. 'Because, I've been selfish, impatient, and now I've ruined everything. The wedding is completely ruined because of me and I don't know what Clara is going to do.' Bella sobbed loudly.

Isabel tilted her head with confusion and so did Clara and Granny Sylta.

'What do you mean you've ruined everything?' her mum asked.

Bella wiped her nose. 'There are no wedding outfits.'

Granny Sylta and Clara exchanged looks of alarm.

'What do you mean there are no wedding clothes? Where are they? What did you do with them?' asked Isabel.

'That day we were supposed to look at the clothes, a ball came over the wall and that's when we met Troy.' Bella explained everything, from the toddler to the key, the flyers, why she was out of the house every day, the lady with the dog, travelling to Greiggs, Mesopotamia, the accidental tour bus ride, and the river rescue.'

'You took the key?' her mum blurted. 'Which lead to you almost losing your lives?'

'The key!' yelled Clara.

Granny Sylta shook her head. 'The key?'

'Bella, how could you go against Clara's wishes?' her mum continued. 'And hide the key story from us. So this is why I haven't been able to do anything with you all since we arrived on the island?'

Bella nervously wrung her hands together and said nothing.

'And whenever I told you that Clara was willing to open the wardrobe to let you see the dresses, you panicked? Because you were hunting down some dog?'

Bella stared at the floor.

'I knew something wasn't right.' Isabel walked back to the breakfast stool and took her seat again. 'But you told me everything was okay. You lied.'

Bella looked at everyone. 'Please don't blame Tommy and Iris, I got them into this mess. The day I took the key Iris begged me not to take it. And Tommy wasn't even with us, but I got him involved. He was in the garden with the baby.' Bella swallowed hard. 'Mum, Clara and Granny Sylta, I'm sorry. I couldn't bear to tell you because I didn't want Clara to worry about not being able to open the wardrobe.'

'Wardrobe?' questioned Isabel. 'But Clara, your Granny Sylta and I were in the wardrobe just two days ago.'

Bella, Iris, and Tommy exchanged confused looks. 'What?' said Iris in shock.

'But Clara said she only had one key,' said Bella.

172

'Yes, I did,' Clara stepped forward. 'But what Kenneth forgot to tell me was he had already cut a spare key two weeks before you arrived on the island, in case it had gotten lost.' Clara's face lit up. 'Thank God for Kenneth, or I don't know what we would have done.'

Bella turned to her friends in disbelief and Tommy banged a fist on his forehead. 'Bella Matthews, what am I going to do with you?'

Iris began to sob again. 'I'm so disappointed.'

'No, Iris, don't be,' Isabel joined in again and looked at Bella. 'This terrible situation had to happen. You have learned that being patient is important. Timing is everything. If you had not taken the key and waited for Clara, you would have seen the dresses the next day. But instead, you were out hunting down that dog. Clara had opened the wardrobe to add another pair of shoes to the collection, but when I contacted you, you said you were in a park eating with Iris and Tommy.'

Iris blinked. 'Oh my goodness, that was the day we spotted the dog for the first time.'

Tommy nodded. 'Yup.'

'So you see Bella,' her mum went on. 'This wedding trip was really meant to teach you about the importance of good listening and patience, and how patience is not meant to slow things down or ruin your fun, but in some cases, it can save your life.'

Iris and Tommy stared at each other.

Bella nodded. 'And a lesson I will never forget.'

Isabel pressed her lips in a firm line. 'And when you get back home Bella, you'll be grounded. Not only will I give away your tickets to the West End show I promised, but you will also be expected to do a month's worth of chores, your mobile phone will be confiscated, no Roblox and Netflix for a month, and lastly …'

Bella knew what was coming. She knew it, the worst of all.

'Litter picking duties until September. Not just in our garden, but in our neighbour's garden too.' finished Isabel, finally.

Bella gave Tommy a side glance. She knew what he was thinking, "savage".

Isabel fixed her gaze on Tommy and Iris now. 'And as for you two, your parents will have to decide what to do once they hear about this monstrosity of a situation.'

Granny Sylta nodded. 'Sure, right.'

Isabel sighed. 'Now all three of you go and have a shower and get ready for bed. Tomorrow is Clara and Kenneth's big day and we all need our beauty sleep. Goodnight kids.'

Bella, Tommy, and Iris quickly spun around and scarpered out of the kitchen.

In silence, their shoes squeaked down the hall when Bella's mind wandered to the dog. Whatever happened to the dog? And how and why did it end up in Clara's yard in the first place?

CHAPTER 37

The next morning Iris attempted for the third time to tie the silk ribbon into a bow around Bella's waist. The bridesmaid dress was everything Bella had imagined and more.

She stood behind Bella and they smiled at their reflections in front of the full-length mirror that was edged with gold.

The colour of their dresses reminded Bella of her favourite raspberry mousse her mum often bought from Tesco's.

Finally knotting the bow, Bella swiped her rose bouquet off the bed and did a twirl. 'This can't be happening. I cannot believe how beautiful we look,' squealed Bella, as they both shimmered in the sunlight.

'Me neither, they are the prettiest dresses I've ever seen,' replied Iris, smoothing down her dress.

The warmth of the morning sun spilled through the large bedroom windows which made patterns on the tiled floor.

A clanking noise from outside caught their attention and they ran up to the window to see the cause of it.

They spotted a large group of workmen assembling a frame, and next to that, a mint green and white marquee.

At the other end of the garden, a band was setting up their instruments and two other men appeared to be doing sound checks on a tiny stage.

'Clara's wedding reception is going to be amazing and later this garden will be filled with so many people,' said Bella.

Iris smiled at that thought but suddenly drew her eyebrows together. 'Oh look, there's Tommy.' She pointed where he stood near a bush and apart from looking smart in a pale blue suit, he appeared to be acting quite suspicious. Iris stared at him. 'What's he up to now?'

'And why is he looking at his watch?' Bella shook her head. 'I wonder whom he's talking to? We don't know anyone on the island apart from Clara and her friends and family.

The girls studied Tommy when suddenly he ran across the lawn, down the garden path, and dashed out the gate.

Bella covered her eyes with her hands. 'I did not see Tommy do that.'

Iris did the same. 'Neither did I.'

Bella removed her hands from her eyes and skipped over to the dressing table. She picked up one of the perfume bottles and sprayed herself and Iris too.

'Apart from tucking into some wedding cake,' said Iris, sniffing the perfume on her wrist. 'I can't wait to see Clara in her dress. In fact, it will be the first time ever I've seen a bride in the flesh. Have you ever seen a bride in real life?' she asked when somebody knocked on their bedroom door.

The door opened and Isabel popped her head in. 'Good morning, how are my two beautiful princesses doing?'

'Mum!' Bella ran up to her and stopped when she took in her mum's outfit.

A floaty peach dress, matching shoes, and a peach broad-brimmed hat. Isabel strutted into the room like she was on a fashion shoot. 'Hello girls,' she grinned. 'Seeing that we have one hour and thirty minutes before we leave, I wanted to check if you were all dressed, and I can see you are.'

'And you look amazing, Isabel,' Iris complimented.

'Thank you, Iris,' she smiled.

Someone else knocked and this time Granny Sylta poked her head in. 'Ladies!' she said, tottering into the bedroom. 'I see we're all ready to go.' Granny was wearing a smart burgundy suit with a matching flower in her long dark hair. Her lipstick, handbag, and shoes matched too and she gave them a twirl.

Bella clapped and gave her granny a bear hug. 'This is so exciting, I almost feel like I'm in a fairy tale. Like Cinderella going to a ball to meet her Prince,' said Bella proudly.

Everyone laughed.

Bella's mum glanced at her watch. 'We need to leave now; the other bridesmaids are waiting downstairs. The bouquets are on the table in the hall, and the cars will be arriving soon.'

'And Clara is the luckiest lady in the world,' added Bella.

Granny Sylta and Iris left the room first, however, Bella stayed behind and looked up into her mum's eyes.

'Mum, I am sorry about last night and what I did. I am so ashamed of myself and I don't even remember making an apology.' Her shoulders flopped.

Isabel cupped her daughter's face and kissed her on the forehead. 'Well you did apologise, you just can't remember. The main thing is you're here, and still alive. Today is a new day. A happy day.'

CHAPTER 38

Every inch of St George's Cathedral in Kingstown was occupied. The melodic chimes of bells rang out above the mosaic of colourful rooftops, swaying palms, and the bustling streets as the first of many guests arrived in style.

They wore the most beautiful colours, satins, and silks that Bella and Iris had ever seen.

As the guests trickled through the grand iron gates, onto the grounds, and up the concrete steps, the wedding party gathered in a burst of colour, laughter, and sweet perfume at the bottom of the steps when Bella and Iris bumped into Troy.

'Hello, girls!' He hugged them and stepped back to admire their dresses. 'You both look *amazing*, like two little princesses,' he complimented.

'Aww, cheers Troy.' Smiled Bella.

'You look amazing too,' said Iris, taking in Troy's smart navy suit and matching shoes.

In his right buttonhole, he wore a pink carnation that matched his tie. 'You have no idea how relieved I was this morning when I peeped out of my bedroom window and caught sight of everyone dressed in wedding clothes in Clara's back garden. I take it you got the key? Thank God you did, I felt awful not being able to go to Greiggs with you guys because of that fishy soup.' He pulled a face. 'Mind you, there is one thing I don't understand, if you went back to the house in Greiggs, how and why on *earth* did you end up in Trinity Falls?'

Iris laughed nervously while Bella smoothed down her dress. 'How we ended up at Trinity Falls is a long story,' explained Bella. 'Why we ended up there is an even longer one, and yes, it's obvious it had something to do with the key.'

'The key we never got,' added Bella.

Troy blinked. 'So how did you get the clothes?'

'Clara had a spare key all this while!' said Iris, throwing her hands in the air as if to say, "enough already!"

Troy rubbed his forehead. 'So you guys ran around the island chasing a dog for a key that you never got, and almost went overboard … for nothing?' His voice squeaked in disbelief.

Bella's face burned with embarrassment. She quickly glanced at the guests nearby in case anyone was listening in. No one seemed to be and was far too excited for Clara's arrival.

'I couldn't believe it when the news story broke on the radio last night,' Troy continued. 'I was thinking, surely, that can't be Bella, Tommy, and Iris from next door, but when the presenter mentioned your names and that you were from the UK, I was like, whaaat?' Troy pulled out a handkerchief from his trouser pocket and dabbed fresh sweat from his face. 'Do you have any idea how far away from Clara's you were? Can any of you swim at all? Do you know how tricky Trinity Falls is?'

'Tricky?' blurted Iris. 'Mission impossible, more like.'

'You had better thank your lucky stars you all lived to tell everyone what happened,' Troy went on. 'It could have been worse, you all could have ended up—'

'Troy.' Bella looked him straight in the eyes. 'Enough. I don't want to hear another thing about Trinity Falls.' She smiled, took a deep breath, and sniffed her pink rose bouquet like it was the last bouquet on earth. 'Today is a new day. A happy day.' She winked, leaned in closer to Troy, and lowered her voice to a whisper. 'I'll fill you in later.'

Iris giggled behind her bouquet.

The grounds of the cathedral grew noisier as more guests arrived. Children chased each other around coconut and mango trees and tried to catch fluttering butterflies bobbing in and out of the blooming hedges.

Cheers erupted when Clara's silver phantom Rolls Royce glided to a stop next to the tall iron gates at the front of the churchyard. It shimmered and sparkled in the Caribbean sunlight when a large group of photographers snapped away that captured every moment.

The maid of honour took this as her cue to gesture to the bridal party to follow her up the steps and take their positions.

Now at the top of the steps, Bella peeped inside at all the guests and spotted Kenneth standing at the front next to his brother and a smiling Reverend Peters.

Kenneth constantly rubbed the back of his neck with worry while glancing at his watch and the main doors.

Bella faced the garden again and watched as Clara stepped out of the car. A glimpse of a tiara, satin shoes, bouquet, and her shimmering veil that floated and sparkled in the afternoon sun. She looked like a dream, a princess from another world.

Iris gasped and covered her hand with her mouth as Clara glided up the long path; a sweeping white gown, puffy sleeves, and a sequined bodice fit for a Queen. 'Somebody, please tell me this is a movie. I'm in a movie, aren't I.' said Iris, making the bridesmaids chuckle.

***

'You may now kiss the bride,' said Reverend Peters two hours later with the biggest smile, and a very sweaty forehead.

Kenneth lifted Clara's veil and did just that.

The guests roared, cheered, and whistled and Bella stuck her fingers in her ears; the noise was as loud as any football match.

Bella scanned the rows of pews and spotted her mum, Granny Sylta, Tommy, Troy, the baby in the onesie whom today was wearing a frilly pink dress, and the other family and friends of Clara's who were all clapping in the front row.

Isabel's phone flashed multiple times as she took photographs, while Granny Sylta turned away from the guests and took a selfie with Bella and the entire wedding party in the background.

Bella squinted and looked closer at Granny Sylta's phone. She was not taking a selfie as she had thought, but instead, she was doing a TikTok live.

Bella keeled over with laughter and nudge Iris in the ribs.

The bright red TikTok "Go Live" button appeared at the bottom of the screen followed by the countdown, and a flurry of comments began to bump up the screen like crazy.

Iris was not able to hold her laughter either and turned to Bella. 'So does that mean Granny Sylta has over one thousand followers?'

'She must do if she's streaming live TikTok videos.' Bella laughed again.

All the guests stood up and the church organ blared out the wedding recessional, signalling for Kenneth and Clara to glide back down the aisle as man and wife.

CHAPTER 39

Back at the villa, the guests gathered in Clara's huge back garden. The music band played Soca music as grown-ups and children danced, ate, chatted, and laughed as waiting staff poured drinks into the shiniest of crystal wear.

Tommy and Troy were sat at one of the many round tables as they tucked into rice, peas, roasted breadfruit, and chicken. The toddler waddled past with a sticky fist and stuffed wedding cake into her mouth.

As the Soca band continued to play, more guests piled into the garden through the side gates and were met by more waiting staff that Clara had hired and passed drinks around on trays.

Kenneth strode into the middle of the garden holding a shiny microphone and called for everyone's attention. 'My wife and I would like to have a group photo with the bridal party, her friends who flew in from England, and our immediate families please.'

'Bella smiled, stood up, and raced across the lawn to meet Iris, Tommy, Granny Sylta, and her mum who had already joined a large group of people gathering at the other end of the garden.

'Iris, Tommy, I thought I'd never find you,' said Bella. 'There's so many people here.'

'We were trying to find you too,' replied Iris.

Although Troy was not a part of the immediate family or friends from England group, he managed to sneak his way into the group photograph. Troy grinned. 'Just wanted to have a photo to look back on to remind me of the time I made some awesome friends from the UK.'

'Awww,' Bella and Iris said at the same time.

'Troy, you are so sweet,' said Bella.

'And we promise, when we leave St Vincent this weekend, that we'll never, ever forget you.'

Troy appeared to be choking back his tears. 'You're leaving this weekend?' he blinked. 'I thought you were going next weekend.' He wiped a tear. 'So you've been on the island for seven days already?'

Iris reached over and hugged him, and so did Bella.

Tommy noted this and joined in the group hug too.

Clara tottered over to everyone; her huge white dress billowing outward. She nestled herself in the middle of the group as the photographer lifted his camera to take the first photo when she held up her hand to stop him. 'Wait, I've just realised Masie is not here.' She looked around the garden. 'Has anyone seen Masie?'

Bella and Iris exchanged excited glances; at last, they were going to meet Masie, and it was about time too.

The other bridesmaids, the ushers, and everyone else posing for a photo scanned the entire back garden when a voice called out from somewhere in the back of the group. 'I found Masie! She's here!' said the voice.

Everyone got back into their positions, however, Bella and Iris craned their necks, eager to see who Masie was. With all the grown-ups towering above them, they could barely see until a man in a purple suit appeared.

Bella and Iris looked at each other confused.

'That can't be Masie,' said Bella

'Isn't that a girl's name?' said Iris.

The photographer motioned for the man in the purple suit to move to the centre of the group.

However, it wasn't until the man was a few steps away that Bella and Iris noticed he wasn't alone. He had a dog on a lead. The dog was dressed in the same colours as the bridesmaids with a pink bow on her head, a sparkly dog collar around her neck, and in her mouth was a toy sausage dog.

'Oh my goodness!' shrieked Bella, 'It's the dog with no name! It's the dog we were looking for!'

Iris's eyes crossed with confusion. 'Masie is the dog with no name? And he... is really... a she?' Iris fanned her face with surprise. 'I can't believe it. I honestly cannot believe it.' Iris nudged Tommy in the ribs who was so lost for words at the revelation, he held his breath.

Troy rubbed his eyes, blinked, and rubbed his eyes again. 'No way,' he said.

The man in the purple suit told Masie to sit for the photograph, and she did.

Finally, the smiling photographer held up his camera and told everyone to say cheese. And like a good little dog, Masie lifted one tiny paw in the air as the camera gave a huge flash.

CHAPTER 40

'Masie belongs to me, she's my dog,' Kenneth revealed to Bella, Tommy, Iris, Troy, Granny Sylta, and Isabel, as they sat beside the swimming pool around one of the larger tables beneath a pink parasol.

The pool was barred off for the occasion that kept the younger children safe.

It was now night time and the air was much cooler.

Reverend Peters helped himself to a plate of wedding cake and took a seat next to his wife.

'The day you arrived on the island I couldn't wait to meet all of you, so as soon as Clara rang to say you had arrived I drove straight down here and brought Masie along for the ride.'

Iris slapped her thigh in recognition. 'Which is why the dog was in the garden that day the key went

189

missing. It wasn't a stray dog as we had thought,' she concluded.

'And the dog was not a dog thief as Bella had suggested,' whispered Tommy, from the side of his mouth to Bella, who nudged him with her elbow.

'So why does Masie have a tag around her neck with the word Greiggs on it when you live here in Cane Garden? And who was that lady that took Masie for walks?' enquired Iris.

Kenneth laughed. 'As of today, I will be living here at the villa with Clara. And that house in Greiggs you said you were spying on, is mine.'

The kids gasped in wonder as Clara joined the group and sat down next to Kenneth with a glass of water.

'As for that lady you saw while trying to hunt down the dog, that is Celine, my dog walker. Celine is from Lyon in France, then moved to St Vincent.'

'So why is she living in St Vincent?' asked Iris.

'Celine came to St Vincent to study; she's an exchange student and took on the job to earn extra money. Plus I needed someone to help walk Masie once the planning of the wedding took all of my time.'

Tommy tilted his head. 'So how about the toy dog? Why does Masie love that dog so much?'

Kenneth sipped on his drink and loosened his tie. 'I adopted Masie from a kill shelter. She was the first dog I saw when I walked in. There she was, lying in a cage and not in the best shape.'

'What do you mean?' Iris straightened Masie's tiny bow on the dog's head.

'She was covered in bruises, patches of hair were missing from her body. She had a cut on one foot and a sore eye.'

Bella bit her lip.

'Her previous owners treated her poorly and she was so alone.' Kenneth went on. 'When I looked in her cage a toy sausage dog was lying next to her.'

Iris made a noise and dabbed her eyes with a napkin.

'The staff told me when they rescued her she never once let go of the toy, and they realised it was her comfort and best friend.'

Troy stroked Masie while Bella hugged her.

'So you saved her life?' asked Iris blinking.

Kenneth nodded. 'And all because I was patient. If I had visited the shelter a week earlier as planned I would have never met Masie because she wasn't at the shelter then.'

'But wouldn't you have adopted another dog if you had gone earlier?' asked Troy.

'Not exactly, the week I had planned to visit, the shelter was closed, and I would have driven thirty miles for nothing. There's no way I would have gone back for a while, and Masie perhaps would not have been given a new home.'

'So you did save her life then, by being patient.' Iris blubbered into her napkin.

'Yes,' said Kenneth. 'I suppose I did.'

Bella's heart sank. Her mum was right. Doing things in a hurry could do more harm than good sometimes. And in this case, a life was saved. This holiday was beginning to make sense to Bella with each passing hour.

'And ever since Masie joined my family, she has been the happiest dog I know.' Kenneth patted Masie on the head.

Bella's heart glowed with a warmth she had never felt before and by the look of everyone else, they felt the same way too.

Tommy stood up and straightened his tie. 'I guess that brings the sausage dog investigation to a beautiful and emotional end.' He clapped his hands together, and everyone laughed. 'I have a surprise of my own too,' Tommy went on. 'And I hope Clara and Kenneth will accept.'

Everyone shared a curious look as they waited for Tommy to explain.

'Hurry up then,' said Bella, rolling her eyes.

Tommy slipped two fingers in his mouth and whistled loudly.

Seconds later another dog wearing a black bow tie around its neck ran up to them and sniffed Masie.

'Oh my goodness, It's him! It's him!' Bella pointed at the dog.

'Who?' asked Granny Sylta, slipping off her glasses to clean them with a napkin.

Iris threw her hands to her cheeks in wonder.

'Do you know this dog?' asked Isabel, narrowing her brows.

'Of course,' Bella laughed. 'This is Casper, Fredrick's dog, the greyhound we visited who we mistakenly thought was Masie.'

Isabel and Granny Sylta exchanged confused glances.

Iris stood up too. 'Tommy, what on earth is going on? How did you get your hands on Casper?'

Tommy cleared his throat. 'When Fredrick mentioned his dad was not well enough to look after the dog, and with Fredrick going off to university and trying to raise funds, I thought of a way to help them. By taking Casper off their hands, his dad wouldn't have to worry about looking after the dog. I divided the reward money of three hundred pounds and gave half to Fredrick for spending money at university and the other half I gave to Thelma for giving us a tip-off, and most importantly ...' Tommy took a deep breath. 'If Casper moves into Clara's house, not only will that stop him from ending up at the shelter, but he and Masie can be best friends for life.'

Everyone sat in silence. An impressed silence.

Iris hugged Masie and Troy did the same.

Bella's thoughts took her back to this morning when she looked out the bedroom window. 'Tommy? Is that why you were on the phone one minute and then dashing out the back garden the next?'

He nodded. 'I arranged to meet Fredrick and Thelma at the front of the house to give them their share of the money, and to bring Casper over. I made Casper a bed in Clara's garage, gave him food, and asked the gardener to keep an eye on him until the wedding was over.'

Isabel and Granny Sylta had a look of pride in their eyes and Troy shook his head in wonderment.

'Tommy Smith.' Troy put his arm around Tommy's shoulders. 'You're one of a kind buddy.'

Iris leaned in to kiss Tommy on the cheek but he playfully brushed it off.

'So, Kenneth and Clara, does that sound like a deal?' Tommy pressed his hands together.

Kenneth scanned everyone's faces and looked at Clara who nodded as she patted Casper.

'We one hundred percent agree, Clara and I would be delighted to give Casper a new home.' He gestured happily around the huge garden that was still heaving with guests. 'At least, we have the room and it's safe here.'

Everyone cheered and patted the dogs as they wagged their tails.

Kenneth shook Tommy's hand. 'Tommy, what you did was so special and selfless, thank you so much.'

Tommy saluted him. 'No problem, Sir.'

'And thank you, everyone,' Kenneth continued, 'for coming all this way to be a part of mine and Clara's special day.'

Isabel nodded. 'It's our pleasure.'

'Don't mention it,' said Granny Sylta, 'we're happy to be here.'

Everyone agreed with a nod when the toddler waddled up to Bella and giggled.

'Hello there,' said Bella to the smiling toddler.

Still giggling, the toddler blinked up at Bella and stretched out a sticky fist that was caked in icing and jam.

Bella laughed and shook her head. 'No mushy wedding cake for me, thank you.'

The toddler opened her tiny hand to reveal something shiny in the centre of her palm.

Bella stared at it. She couldn't believe it. It was the missing wardrobe key. 'The key!' Bella shrieked. 'The missing key!'

'The key?' asked Iris, confused.

Bella's outburst caused Tommy and everyone else to look up sharply.

'What do you mean the key?' Iris went on, and with the rest of the family gathering around.

Granny Sylta sat up straighter and fixed her hat. 'Don't tell me this was the key you were looking for.'

Everyone's gaze now shifted to granny.

'You knew about the key?' Bella asked Granny. 'We thought it was in Maisie's toy dog all this while. Where did you see it?'

'The day we arrived I remember seeing the baby playing with it next to the paddling pool and in the house.' Granny Sylta pointed to the far side of the garden. 'You see that rose bush over there?'

Everyone's eyes followed.

'The key would be swinging on those branches as she played with it.'

'The rose bush?' said Bella, now facing Tommy with a stern look.

Tommy shrugged nervously. 'I'm sure the toddler put the key in the toy dog. She did. I saw her.'

'She must have taken it out when you weren't looking for the key to having ended up on a rose bush,' chimed in Iris. 'How did we miss that? And Clara and Isabel too?'

Clara shook her head. 'Beats me.'

'She'd often play with the key when the three of you were out and about,' added Granny. 'And at night time, she would drop it into her toys.'

A hum of chatter broke out among everyone and Isabel lifted her hands. 'Everyone, please, at the end of the day, if the key was left in the vase as instructed.' Isabel fixed her eyes on Bella. 'None of this would have happened. According to what Granny has said, it appeared the key never left the house.'

'And which is why the key never fell out on the boat at Trinity Falls,' concluded Tommy.

Troy scratched his head. 'And all three of you could have gone overboard into the river … for nothing.'

'It didn't cross my mind to mention anything to anyone about the key.' Granny took a sip of her juice. 'As far as we were concerned, nothing was missing, Clara had a spare key and there was no need to raise an alarm.'

Tommy shook his head in wonder and so did Troy.

'The main thing is.' Isabel stood up. 'No matter how this holiday may have turned out, some of us have something important to take away with us.' She shifted her gaze to Bella and her friends. 'So let's celebrate and enjoy ourselves while we're here, after all, this is Clara and Kenneth's big day, remember?'

And just like that, the band began to play an up-tempo song, but now with steel pans. Kenneth quickly scanned the garden. 'Isabel is right, and that's our cue for a dance with my beautiful wife.'

Clara smiled around at everyone. 'Enjoy the rest of the night, have fun, and I'll see you all later,' she smiled, before walking off hand in hand with Kenneth.

Isabel and Granny Sylta loved the sound of the steel pan music too and shuffled over to where everyone was dancing.

Tommy pulled Iris onto the dance floor and they twirled and laughed together.

Troy was up on his feet too as he danced with the toddler who had changed into a shiny silver onesie.

Bella now sat alone with the dogs as they wandered around her feet. She watched the joy of the reception party with memories of her time on the island filling her mind. A feeling of sadness came over her knowing that in a few days she would no longer be here. However, the sadness was soon replaced with a feeling of joy as she looked forward to telling her friends and neighbours back home about her holiday; how her trip to St Vincent and the Grenadines was the most amazing, funniest, revealing, and scariest Caribbean adventure… ever!

She smiled at the dogs and stood up. 'Come here Masie, come here girl.' She held Masie's two paws as Casper pranced around their feet. And this made Masie, Casper, and Bella jump with glee. 'Let's dance!'

THE END

THANK YOU

We would love to thank everyone who has bought a paperback copy or an ebook copy of this book. We would also love to thank our friends, family, and book bloggers who supported the launch, took part in our virtual Bella's Big Caribbean Adventure Book Tour launch party, and shared our book on their social media and WhatsApp platforms.

Special thanks to our editor, Soulla Christodoulou. Again, it's been great working with you on another adventure with Bella, Tommy, and Iris. Here's to more adventures!

If you have reached the end of the paperback version of this book, kindly head over to Amazon and leave us a short review.

It does not have to be long.

We look forward to hearing your thoughts. Thank you for reading.

Lots of love, Anne and Annabelle X

About the Authors

Vincentian-descendents, Mum and daughter duo are the authors of the Bella Series, the first book being Bella's Christmas Wonderland Adventure, formally known as Lost in Christmas Wonderland.

Annabelle has always loved to write and began when she was very young. When at home, Annabelle and her brother love to bake cookies and go for walks. Her favourite authors are Alesha Dixon, Serena Patel, Tamzin Merchant, and the list keeps growing.

Having been to St Vincent many times as a child, Anne knew one day she would love to write about the island and how beautiful it is. Anne began her creative writing journey in 2007 where she pantsed many stories, read heaps of how-to writing books before attending part-time classes at the City Lit. Since then, she has immersed herself within the online writing community and started a book blog back in 2013 called Books and Authors. During this time to keep herself in the loop, she regularly visited The London Book Fair, (and still does) connected with more authors, and later went on to publish a three-part series, two children's books, and a puzzle and activity book.

There will be more adventures from Bella and friends. Stay in touch and look us up on Instagram.

More Caribbean Adventures

Join Bella, Tommy, and Iris For More Adventures In This Fun-Packed Activity And Colouring Book.

Based on the storybook, each page is filled with lots of different activities including a secret island mysteries puzzle, a maze, word searches, and interesting facts about St Vincent.

This fun activity and colouring book would make a lovely gift, to take on holiday, or when you have some downtime. So get ready and hang out with Bella, Tommy, and Iris for another Big Caribbean Adventure!

Available on Amazon

When ten-year-old Bella Matthews and her mum, Isabel, visit Granny Sylta in the snowy village of Lakersfield for Christmas, it turns out there is more in store than just Christmas cake and a ton of presents.

When she arrives, she meets her cousin Rita and a boy called Tommy for the first time and catches up with her friend Iris again too. Together they discover an exciting attraction is in town: A giant Christmas Wonderland Theme Park. They are dazzled by hundreds of decorated Christmas trees, a Musical Nativity, a Santa Parade, an Upside Down House, and many more attractions.

But Bella ends up having an unexpected adventure of her own as she dances with pot-bellied Santas, discovers a palace made entirely out of glass, wanders into an intriguing puzzle room, and treks for miles to find shelter on a snowy night.

Can Bella find her way back to Granny Sylta's house in time for Christmas dinner?

Bella's Christmas Wonderland Adventure is a story about courage, kindness, friendship, the importance of family, and the magic of Christmas.

Bella was in a trance. She stared in wonder at the scale of everything. It was much bigger than a football field; more like a magical forest filled with the tallest Christmas trees, she had ever seen. The trees were all dressed up in thousands of twinkling fairy lights and bows and there were adults and children everywhere.

It had nearly been an hour since they arrived. Bella, Rita, and Tommy had so far screamed their lungs out on Santa's flying sleigh, spooked by the Haunted Mansion, whirled in the Giant Tea Cup Ride, dazzled by the Wonderland Circus, and shared many giggles on the North Pole Ice Rink where they tried to skate while holding onto the handrail around the edge and falling onto their bottoms.

'I don't ever want to skate again,' laughed Bella, pulling off her skating boots and waiting for the others to hand theirs back.

After leaving the ice rink, they made their way through the crowds. Above them was a large canopy of Christmas stockings, candy canes, and dried orange slices dangling above them. Then the delightful smells of mince pies and hot dogs tingled their noses as they walked past the busy stalls that lined an illuminated pathway leading to a sign that said Santa's Village.

'Have you ever seen anything like it?' Bella asked the others, but no one answered.

Loudspeakers blared out Christmas carols overhead, and the Snow Queen Roller Coaster hovered then roared into motion high above their heads, swooshing into a blend of silver and white.

As Tommy and Rita took in the sights, only then did Bella understand why Rita said she could easily get lost here. What a place to get lost in!

Rita put her arm around Bella's tiny shoulders and hugged her.

They followed a sign that read, *"The Glass Palace - This Way"*. The sign led them through a garden full of shiny gold and silver baubles and acorns sprayed with fake snow, attached to long green stalks that sparkled under the fairy lights.

Bella reached out to touch a bauble; it was cool and smooth. 'Awesome!' she cried. 'Who would have thought baubles and snow-sprayed acorns would make such pretty flowers?'

'Or fruit?' said Tommy, picking one and giving it to Bella.

'Tommy?' Bella's eyes widened. She looked around and stuffed the bauble into her pocket.

Rita stopped to take a picture of the garden then posed for a selfie. 'Flowers or fruit, either way, it's a beautiful place.'

Reaching the end of the garden, The Glass Palace appeared like magic as it rose from among the Christmas trees and stood opposite them. For a moment, Bella believed she had entered a storybook or some faraway fantasy land, and no one could convince her otherwise.

BELLA **S**ERIES AVAILABLE ON **A**MAZON

Books & AUTHORS Publishing ^{UK}

Printed in Great Britain
by Amazon

17743683R00130